CW01021672

An English
Village Fairy Tale

First edition

This edition published in 2022

 Designed and typeset by
HULLO CREATIVE

www.hullocreative.com

Copyright © Toots Malton 2022

All rights reserved. No portion of this book may be reproduced, stored in a retrieval system, or transmitted in any form or by any means, (mechanical, electronic, photocopying, recording, or otherwise), without written permission from the copyright owner and publisher.

Illustrations by Deenagh Miller

ISBN 978-1-8382903-1-3

An English Village Fairy Tale

Dunster is so magical,
might it hold a secret deep within its heart?
Do wishes really come true?

Toots Malton

Contents

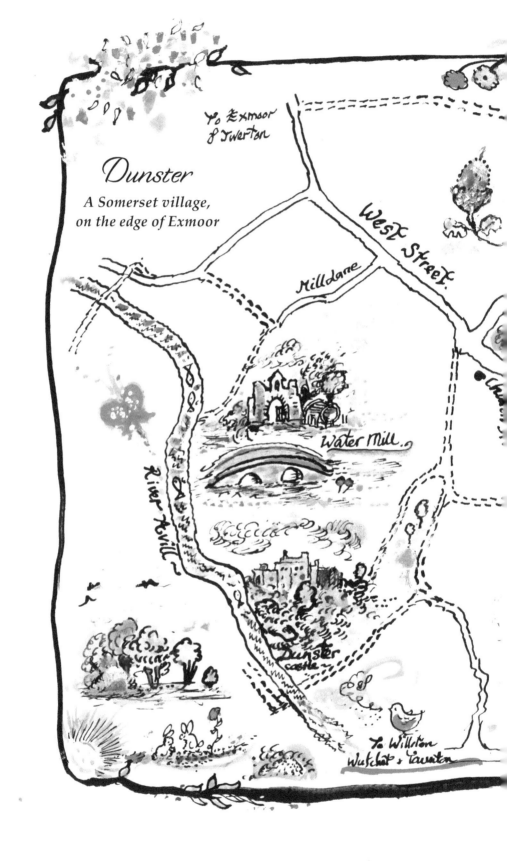

Dunster

A Somerset village,
on the edge of Exmoor

To Exmoor
& Iwerton

West Street

Milldane

Water Mill

River Avill

Dunster
castle

To Williton
Watchet & Taunton

To Alcombe & Minehead

St George's Street

Dove Cote

Wishing Well

nster urch

~ YARN Market ~

High Street

Conygne Tower

Conygne Woods.

Dunster Steep

To Minehead & Porlock

Path to Dunster Marsh Beach

Chapter 1

Do you believe in fairies?

Our story begins with a little girl called Henrietta Isabella. She was named Henrietta after her Great Grandmother — a beautiful name, but a little long don't you think? So her friends and family just called her 'Hetty'.

Hetty was an only child. She adored spending time reading her books and writing stories. She would try to write a new story each week ready for the weekend, as Sunday was the day Hetty would be visiting her Grandma for afternoon tea.

Granny lived in what was once quite a grand old country house on the edge of a pretty village. Hetty loved to play in the garden, with its narrow winding paths, secret hiding places, sweet smelling roses shrubs and trees. Although, sitting by the fish pond was her most favourite place. She adored watching the dragonflies hover over the water lilies, their silver and sapphire blue wings gleaming in the bright sunlight. There was something so enchanting and magical about them, almost like little fairies dancing and fluttering all around. Hetty always wished that one day she might be lucky enough to actually meet a real little fairy. As Granny's garden seemed the most perfect place for little fairies to live. Hetty peeked into every corner and under every bush — just like she always did. But there was never a fairy to be found.

Feeling hungry, and a little disappointed, she slowly wandered back to the house where Granny's perfect tea would be waiting. That was sure to cheer her up.

The enormous kitchen table was covered with a bright red and white gingham tablecloth. Sitting in the middle, on a beautiful glass cake stand, was Granny's (truly delicious) chocolate cake, with loads of chocolate cream in the middle and chocolate buttons on the top.

After tea, everyone enjoyed snuggling down on the cosy sofas in the sitting room, and Hetty read one of her stories to her Grandma. It was a tale of magical far away places, where animals and fairies could talk, dance, and fly.

"Well, my dear, what imagination you have," said Grandma, when Hetty had finished reading.

Hetty was very puzzled, "Granny do you believe in fairies?"

"Well goodness me, my dear child, I most certainly do."

Hetty's brown eyes suddenly grew wider and wider.

"You see, little one, not everything is always as it seems. Sometimes if you truly believe in something, one day quite out of the blue your wishes might just come true."

"Honestly Mother, I wish you would stop filling her head full of silly nonsense," said Hetty's Mummy, "we seem to have fairies from morning to night."

"Nothing wrong with that" said Grandma, giving Hetty a knowing wink.

"Well Granny, if you say it's true then it must be. I will just have to keep wishing and wishing that's all. Who knows, maybe one day as you say, my wishes might just come true..."

Later that evening, after such a lovely day, Hetty gave her Mummy and Daddy a goodnight kiss, snuggled down into her warm bed with her beloved teddy tucked firmly under her arm, and soon she was fast asleep.

Hetty and her parents were very happy living in their small cosy house. Daddy loved working in his garden, and growing beautiful roses was the thing he enjoyed most of all. Hetty sometimes liked to help water the tomatoes in the greenhouse or plant flower seeds into little pots. But one day, quite out of the blue, Daddy asked if Hetty would like to use the old shed at the bottom of the garden.

"Yes please, Daddy, that would be wonderful," she replied.

Soon it was cleared of all the rubbish that always seems to collect in old sheds, the floor was covered with a bright colourful rug. Mummy added a small round table, two wooden chairs, then to finish, some bright cheerful curtains.

It was brilliant.

At last, Hetty had her very own playhouse with plenty of room for books, toys, but (most importantly) her enormous dressing up box. Inside, carefully wrapped in soft white tissue paper, was Hetty's most treasured possession: a beautiful deep purple velvet cape, adorned with sequins and sparkling crystals. It had once belonged to Hetty's Great Grandmother. It was very, very old and smelt of mothballs (in fact, all of Granny's wardrobe smelt of mothballs). Even so, it was the most beautiful thing Hetty had ever seen. She would wrap it around herself, then parade up and down the garden using an old wooden spoon as a wand. It was fun having her friends over, as they would spend hours dressing up, playing with their dolls, making up stories or dancing around the lawn.

Hetty loved to draw pictures of fairies. She longed for the day she might actually meet a real little fairy. The boys who lived next door love to tease her, calling out "there are no such thing as silly fairies". They would run around their garden flapping their arms up and down pretending they could fly.

"Oh please stop being so horrid. My Grandma has told me that she believes in fairies so that is good enough for me. I just have to keep wishing and wishing, that's all."

Why are boys so daft? she thought to herself, they don't know anything. Kicking a silly football around and making a nuisance of themselves is all they seem to do. Girls do much nicer things.

I am really glad I don't have any silly brothers, they would just make me very cross.

Hetty and her friends belonged to a dancing school, their class took place every Saturday morning in a large wooden building. All sorts of things were held there: jumble sales, Boy Scout meetings, sometimes cake and coffee mornings, often a band would play so grown-ups could hold dances on Friday or Saturday nights. But Saturday mornings were just for ballet and tap lessons. The wooden floor was just perfect, everyone would make as much noise as they could with their tap shoes.

It was quite a long walk to the dancing class, on the way Hetty would meet up with her friends. Sometimes they had to run to get there on time, as their dance teacher was very strict and did not allow anyone to be late for her class. "Slapdash time keeping is exceedingly bad manners" she would say in a very loud high pitched voice with her glasses perched firmly on the end of her nose. When she was cross, her face would go bright red, then she would often bang her stick up and down on the floor in time to the music — it was extremely hard not to have a fit of the giggles.

The huge upright piano stood proudly in the corner of the hall, it was played by a very old lady called Mrs Evans. She always dressed in long skirts, teamed with layers of brightly coloured hand knitted jumpers or cardigans, rounded off with a funny little red hat held in place with an array of hat pins. It would wobble and wobble around when she was playing a fast piece of music, but somehow the little red hat always managed to stay firmly on her head. After the class, she would search through the huge tapestry bag she always kept on a chair next to her. It was full of all sorts of things; knitting wool, needles, music books, several pairs of glasses, and goodness knows what else. Then out would come a large bag of sweets and she would kindly offer one to each of the children.

Sometimes Hetty and her friends would arrive early for their class so they would sit on the steps leading up to the hall. From there, they could see through the railings to the railway station. Often a train would go rumbling past. Hetty adored travelling on the train and longed for her summer holiday, but it did seem such a long way off on a grey wet day.

Finally, after what seemed like forever, it was the last day of term. The Headmaster gave his usual very, very long speech.

"Now children, off you go enjoy your summer holiday, I will look forward to seeing you all again next term."

Phew! At last it was over.

The children were just so happy, at last, there was six whole weeks of fun to enjoy.

Little did Hetty know her magical summer holiday was about to begin…

Chapter 2

Mr Christmas

Hetty was born in 1945, so that made her just ten years old. There wasn't a lot of money around after the war, you just had to 'make do and mend'. That's just how it was. Houses were kept warm with coal fires — no central heating and cosy bedrooms like you have now. A warm nightdress or pyjamas, your teddy bear and a hot water bottle was as good as it got. You never knew whether to warm up your tummy or your toes.

Sometimes on very cold winter mornings, there would be deep snow outside and ice on the inside of Hetty's bedroom window. She would leap from her bed then rush down to the warmth of the kitchen, snuggled up in her dressing gown and slippers. The kitchen was the warmest place in the house, as there was always a cosy fire burning in the old kitchen range.

But now it is summer, the snow and the cold winter left far behind... and time for us to continue with our story.

Hetty slowly opened her eyes, the sun was shining brightly through her bedroom window. She smiled as she watched her pretty curtains dancing in the warm summer breeze.

Today was a very special day. The day she had been longing for.

At last, Hetty would be going on holiday for two weeks to stay with her Aunty Lily and Uncle Jim. They lived in a beautiful medieval village right on the edge of Exmoor called Dunster, with its cobbled pavements, cosy thatch cottages, teashops and so much more.

Dunster village is nestled between two hills. On the top of the first hill sits Dunster Castle. Hetty thought it looked just like a magical fairytale castle encircled by the dense castle woods. The village children found it the most perfect place to play hide-and-seek — it was dark and scary, with the added excitement of hoping they wouldn't be caught sneaking around in the private castle grounds.

On top of the second hill you will find Conygar Tower, it's just an empty ruin now except for the black rooks who have made it their home. Even today if you visit the village, listen. You will still be able to hear them squawking high above the tower, swooping and swirling around the tree tops.

The old village Church is still such a lovely place, so quiet cool and peaceful on a hot summers day. With the aisles full of vases overflowing with sweet smelling summer flowers (or holly at Christmas), lovingly arranged by the village ladies.

Behind the Church you will find a very pretty walled garden. Hetty always called it her 'secret magic garden', because in the garden is a wishing well.

After you have made your wish, take a peep out through the little wooden door at the end of the garden. There you will find a tall round building. This is the old village Dovecote. Who knows, perhaps it might hold a secret in this village fairy tale?

At the top of the village is the Yarn Market, a large round building with open sides. Once a week tables would be set up inside and out on the cobbled pavements. Saturday was market day and people would bring along all sort of things to sell — vegetables, cakes, books, home-made jam and so much more.

Many folk lived out on the moors or on remote Exmoor farms, so they always enjoyed coming into the village once a week to shop or even just to catch up on all the village news.

Often, colourful Morris Dancers would dance through the village with jangling bells around their ankles, shaking tambourines or banging drums. The children loved to skip after the dancers, clapping their hands to the music. Holiday folk would enjoy ice creams, or a visit to the castle. It was just so magical sitting high up on the hill.

The old farmers, though, were not into all that dancing stuff. They would creep off to a village pub to enjoy a few flagons of beer or cider.

"Too much than what is good for them," Aunty Lily would say, "makes them start telling fanciful tales about things they see in the woods, and out on the moors — strange and mysterious things.

But anyway, I think it's just a load of gibberish. Old tittle-tattle, that's all it is, I am sure of it. Nothing but old wives tales."

Exmoor has held so many haunting tales for hundreds of years. Its steep valleys are often covered with a dense cloak of mist, howling wind or deep winter snow. In springtime, the moors come alive once more — glowing with bright yellow gorse, then later pink, white and purple heather.

Now, midsummer skylarks will be singing high up in the sky, sheep will just be lazily wandering around grazing on the sweet smelling grass. Hetty adored the Exmoor ponies, and helping her Aunty Lily pick sweet tasting berries (later to be baked into a pie enjoyed with delicious cream).

After remembering all these things, Hetty just couldn't wait a moment longer. She dashed into her bedroom, just in time to see the last few things being packed into a huge red case.

"Just a minute, Mummy. I must take my old teddy with me, I am sure he would enjoy a holiday too."

Hetty's Mummy laughed, "Your poor old teddy has seen better days. Maybe one day I might make him a smart new red jacket, with bright shiny brass buttons and soft green velvet trousers."

"That would be so lovely," said Hetty, "but he will just have to come as he is for now."

"Hetty, are you sure you need to take all these things?"

"Oh yes. You see, if it rains, I will be able to write lots of new stories and read them to Aunty Lily and Uncle Jim."

Just then, Daddy appeared at the door.

"Now then, young lady, make sure you don't wear poor Aunty and Uncle out, they are not as young as they used to be. We must all be on our way, I don't want you to miss your train."

Hetty adored staying at her Aunty and Uncle's. They lived in a very old cottage with only a short walk to the beach. Its thick walls always kept the cottage feeling nice and cool inside, even on a very hot summers day. The sitting room had tiny little windows with wooden shutters, and wide comfy window seats — the perfect place to sit and quietly read, or just watch the birds in Uncle Jim's garden enjoying tidbits from the bird table.

Hetty thought the huge inglenook fireplace was wonderful too. It had a seat built in on either side of the fire. Just imagine how cosy it would be to sit there in the wintertime — warming up your toes, perhaps toasting marshmallows or chestnuts at Christmas. Last summer, Hetty had crawled right into the fireplace (when the fire was out, of course!) and peered up through the chimney. It was so wide she could see right up to the sky, and the chimney echoed back to her when she called out "hello".

Hidden behind a small latch door, steep rickety stairs curved up to a large landing with three bedrooms — two large ones, and a very pretty single room. This was where Hetty would be sleeping. The bathroom, on the other hand, was downstairs just off the kitchen, and it had the most enormous bath Hetty had ever seen.

Last year, Uncle Jim had made her a swing tied from the branches of an apple tree. It really was the best place ever, and just to think that Hetty would soon be there to enjoy two whole weeks in the little cottage by the sea.

Aunty Lily spent most of her time in the kitchen. She loved baking cakes and would often win a prize at the village fête for her strawberry jam, made from Uncle Jim's delicious strawberries.

They owned a very funny little dog called Smudge, named so because he had a tiny little white patch on the side of his nose. He loved to bark and chase the rabbits around the garden. He was always such a happy little dog, his tail would waggle and waggle. One day he caught a wasp and it bit him on the mouth, so after that horrible experience he now just keeps to chasing rabbits or the odd butterfly.

Next door to Aunty Lily and Uncle Jim lived Mrs Green and her husband. They had a daughter called Anne who was a good friend of Hetty's Mummy. Anne had twin daughters named Beth and Ruth. Hetty always found it hard to tell them apart, but when the girls were down last summer they all had loads of fun.

So it was such a lovely surprise when Hetty was told the girls would be down again for this holiday. Goodness, thought Hetty, it will be so exciting to see them again!

The station was very busy when they arrived.

Daddy gave Hetty a big hug. "Now then, young lady, make sure you don't get into any mischief. I must say it will be strange and so very quiet not having you around for a while, little one."

Hetty kissed him on both cheeks then one on his forehead for luck.

"Now be off with you, and make sure you write to let us know how you are."

"I will, Daddy, I promise. Goodness I am so excited!"

Just then a porter came hurrying along to help with their luggage. The intoxicating smell of steam trains, oil smoke and sealing wax filled the air. People were busy making their way to various platforms to await their train. Hetty could feel the air just buzzing with excitement.

"Mummy, don't you think stations are the most wonderful exciting places?"

There was just so much noise. Porters pushed trolleys piled high with luggage, milk churns, even large baskets full of racing pigeons.

Hetty stopped to say hello to a lady with her little baby in a huge pram. The baby was wearing a blue sun hat so Hetty thought it must be a little boy.

"He is very sweet baby."

"Well, thank you," said the lady. She asked if Hetty had any brothers or sisters.

"Oh no, it's just Mummy and Daddy and me."

Goodness, Hetty thought, that might change one day! Who knows, perhaps a little brother or sister might come along. She had never thought about this before. Hetty thought about how horrid the boys next door could be, and wondered if they were sweet little babies once.

"That would be very nice," she said to herself thoughtfully, "but if it happens, I hope it's a little sister. I don't like big boys very much, that's for sure."

Suddenly, a group of Boy Scouts came onto the platform carrying huge rucksacks and making such a lot of noise. Lucky things, thought Hetty, they must be going camping. I have never slept in a tent before, that must be so much fun. Daddy told me he used to go camping when he was a Boy Scout, maybe we could try it sometime.

Hetty asked her Mummy if she could walk to the end of the platform to wait for the train.

"Yes, but do be careful. Make sure you keep well away from the edge. I can keep an eye on you from here, but you must come back as soon as you see the train in the distance."

"I promise, Mummy, there are just so many exciting things to see."

Hetty noticed there were lots of other children going on holiday too, looking very excited as they waited for their train surrounded by bags, cases, buckets and spades.

Moving away from the lady with her baby, Hetty wandered further along the platform. I wonder where all these people will be staying on holiday, she thought. Perhaps a caravan or even a beach hut.

There are beach huts on Dunster beach. Sometimes Hetty's parents would rent one for a week or so, right on the edge of the sea. It was the most perfect place to enjoy a summer holiday. Only this year, Hetty would be staying at her Aunty and Uncle's cottage instead. She didn't mind, as this would allow her to play with the children who lived in the village, also Beth and Ruth. She was just longing to see them again.

Hetty smiled at a very smartly dressed elderly Lady and Gentleman sitting on a bench gently holding hands. The gentleman was wearing a very smart Panama hat, a cream linen jacket with a red rose pined into the lapel. The lady looked so lovely in a beautiful pink summer dress, a cream straw hat with dainty pink flowers around the brim. They didn't look as if they were going on holiday, so maybe just a day trip. Probably to the seaside to enjoy an ice cream or even a lovely cream tea, to just remember when they first met and fell in love.

I wonder if when I grow up I might fall in love. Perhaps I might wear a beautiful white wedding gown, with flowers in my hair, or even marry a handsome prince. Then just like in the fairy tales we would both live happily ever…

Hetty soon snapped out of her thoughts when she bumped into someone.

"Now steady on, young lady, you were miles away, so deep in thought not to notice me."

Hetty glanced up, squinting against the sun, and found herself gazing up at a tall gentleman wearing a floppy old hat. He had very long white hair and a long white beard. She gave a confused smile.

"I am very sorry, I just wasn't looking where I was going."

"Don't worry," he said in a gentle voice. "Well, young lady, you look as if you might be going on your summer holiday, all dressed in your shorts and sun hat."

"Yes, that's right. My name is Hetty, I am going to visit my Aunty and Uncle. I will be staying with them for two weeks in their little cottage by the sea. I feel very excited, it will all be so lovely and wonderful, don't you think? Mummy is taking me, she's sitting on the bench over there. Goodness, I just love going on holidays don't you?"

"Well, I do think it all sounds, as you say, quite wonderful and very exciting indeed." Said the old gentleman. "I have noticed there are many other happy little children waiting for the train, now I am quite sure, dear Hetty, you are all going to enjoy a most happy and delightful time."

Hetty took a step back out of the sun, she could then see the gentleman had a big round tummy and a happy smiling face. He was also quite old and reminded her of someone.

"Excuse me sir, are you going on your holiday too? Only you don't seem to have any luggage."

"Oh, I never need luggage," said the gentleman. "I am just here on a little business trip, that's all, and thought it would be rather nice to travel by train for a change. You see, it is quite different from my usual form of transport."

"I see," said Hetty, rather puzzled.

"I do hope you have a lovely holiday, young lady. Enjoy the sunshine, it will soon be winter again, you see. I have a lot to do before then, lots of orders to place and things to sort out. I must say it all keeps me very busy."

"Look everyone! The train is coming!" Called out one of the Boy Scouts.

"Gosh! I must go," said Hetty.

"It has been very nice talking to you, my dear," said the gentleman, "now watch where you are going this time."

"I will, thank you." Said Hetty, quickly running back along he platform.

"Who were you talking with?" Her Mummy asked.

"It was just a man on a business trip. But it does seem very odd, don't you think? You see, he has no luggage — not even a briefcase like Daddy when he goes away on business. Goodness, he reminds me of someone, but I just cannot think who it is."

"Well, if you ask me," said Mummy, "I think he looks just like Father Christmas. After all he does have long white hair, a long white beard, and a big round tummy."

"That's it!" Exclaimed Hetty. "I knew he reminded me of someone! Mummy do you think he could be Father Christmas?"

"Goodness, Hetty, what will you think of next? You are just as bad as your Grandma with all your crazy thoughts!"

"Well, Mummy, do you remember when we were last at Grannies? She said 'things may not be always as they seem', well I think it could be true. What if it is Father Christmas? Why would he be here on a business trip? Oh heavens, it is all so very confusing."

"Never mind all that for now, we have a train to catch. Come on, young lady, pick up your things."

Hetty glanced back along the platform. I wish I knew where he was going, she thought. I will just have to keep looking out of the window each time the train stops at a station. I wonder if I will have a chance to find out more. It's all such a mystery. But for now, I am just going to have to call him…

MR CHRISTMAS

The Station Master blew his whistle, then began moving people back from the edge of the platform.

Hetty could see the train in the distance, gleaming in the bright summer sunshine. How wonderful it looked with steam swirling all around, and smoke billowing out from the chimney, leaving a huge white trail across the blue summer sky. How exciting it must be to be a train dashing through the open countryside, through towns and villages, on and on to yet another destination.

As the train entered the station, the engine driver blew the whistle. It was so loud it made Hetty jump, quickly clasping her hands over her ears.

The train continued to rumble along the platform, its brakes hissing and squealing as it struggled to slow down. Finally, it shuddered to a loud screeching halt, as the brakes were pulled on it seemed to give out an enormous sigh. As suddenly a whoosh of hot steam came gushing out from beneath the engines huge shiny black belly, engulfing everyone on the platform in a cloud of soft warm mist. Then it slowly cleared, floating gently up and away. The sun shone through once more.

Hetty smiled to herself. At last, her holiday was about to begin.

Quickly glancing back along the platform, she was curious to see where Mr Christmas would be boarding the train. There he is, she thought. And as if he knew she was watching, he turned to look at her, raised his hat and gave her a little wave.

Then he was gone.

"Come on, Hetty," said Mummy "I hope we can find a seat — look there's room in this carriage. Now you go and sit by the window."

Hetty watched as milk churns, parcels, baskets of racing pigeons, Boy Scout tents, bikes and heaps of other things were loaded into the guard's van. Last of all, the huge pram was safely placed on board. The guard now made sure, with a series of very loud bangs, that all the doors were firmly closed.

Gently, the steam engine tugged at the carriages. Puff, puff, went the engine slowly, slowly they started to move along the platform. Making everyone gently rock backwards and forwards in their seats, as they crept past the old hut where Hetty enjoyed her dancing class. She remembered sitting on the steps watching the trains go by longing for this day.

This was it at last. She was on her way.

Little did Hetty know her wonderful magical holiday was about to begin...

Chapter 3

On the train

Finally free from the station, the train started to gather speed. The engine driver blew the whistle, Hetty thought the train seemed very happy to be on its way again. Within moments, they were out in the countryside, now the carriages started to rock gently from side to side. Hetty leant back in her seat, closing her eyes. She loved the sound the wheels made on the track…

Clickity clack, clickity clack
Went the wheels on the
Railway track
Pass meadows, fields and farms
And the old scarecrow with waving arms
On and on we go
Quite fast then sometimes slow
Smoke from the engine drifting by

Leaving white streamers in the sky

Passing sleeping cows

And fluffy sheep

Stopping at stations with odd

Sounding names

Over bridges and winding lanes

Until at last, what do we see?

High red cliffs

And shimmering sea...

"Look Mummy it's the sea! I can see the sea!"

All through the journey, each time the train stopped at a station Hetty peered out of the window to see if Mr Christmas was getting off, but so far he must be still on the train.

The guard moved through the carriages, calling out loudly "Blue Anchor, Blue Anchor, next stop".

Hetty gazed out of the window as suddenly the beach came into view.

"Look Mummy, the tide is in. Goodness, I am so excited!"

The train finally screeched then shuddered to a halt. The guard's van door was opened, where the very excited Boy Scouts gathered around to collect their bags and tents. But first they had to wait for the huge pram to be gently placed onto the platform, where the lady and her baby were waiting.

Heavens, thought Hetty, I hope the boys don't have to walk too far with all their things it all looks very heavy. Even so, camping must be brilliant fun.

Well, she thought, the Boy Scouts, the lady and baby plus lots of other people are getting off the train, but Mr Christmas must still be on board.

"Only two stops to go before the train will arrive at Minehead," said Mummy, "now that is the end of the line, so we get off at the next station."

"Mummy, I do hope Uncle Jim has remembered we are coming today."

"Oh don't you worry. According to Aunty Lily, he has been talking about it for weeks. He loves having you around, it keeps him feeling young, or so he says."

With the doors firmly closed, once more the train huffed puffed and rattled happily along the track.

"Dunster, next stop Dunster." Called the guard.

"Come on Hetty, now, gather up your things."

The train started to slow down, after a lot of hissing and brakes squealing, it finally shuddered then jolted to a sudden halt.

Hetty glanced out the window to see if she could see Uncle Jim, instead Mr Christmas went hurrying past.

Oh heavens bother, thought Hetty. I've missed him.

Leaping from the train, Hetty ran along the platform. There was Uncle Jim holding out his arms to catch her.

"My goodness, young lady, bless my soul you've grown some since I saw you last! And as pretty as a picture, just like your Mummy and Grandma. Now, I best go and give your Ma a hand with all your things. I can see you have brought the sunshine with you too, now that's a good thing, don't you think? Always good for the sun to shine for a lovely holiday by the sea."

"Hello May, I must say, 'tis so good to see you again."

"It's good to see you too, Uncle Jim," replied Hetty's Mummy, "Goodness me, I must say you're looking very smart."

"Well, my dear May, 'tis like this, you see, old Ted the local taxi driver has been none too well of late. So until he gets back on his feet again, your Aunty Lily says I have to help him out, so here I am all dressed up and looking like a stuffed turkey at

Christmas. Mind you, it makes quite a pleasant change from working in my greasy old garage, that's for sure. Sometimes I pick up them posh folks from the hotels for a drive out across Exmoor, then perhaps later a visit to Minehead or Porlock — well, I must say, dear May, I've been finding it all most enjoyable."

Uncle Jim helped Hetty and her Mummy with their luggage.

"And another thing," he continued, "them posh ladies smells lovely. 'French perfume' they calls it, 'tis much nicer then the smell of petrol or oil in my garage. The tips aren't bad either, we reckon that old Ted as been onto a good thing all these years. It means your Aunty Lily has been able to treat herself to a new frock or two, now that can't be a bad thing. She thinks she is quite a lady these days — all dressed up and nowhere to go."

He paused and looked around. "Now then, where has that little maid Hetty gone? There she is, what are you looking for young-in? With a face like that you look as though you have lost a shilling and found a sixpence."

"I have lost my Mr Christmas," said Hetty in a worried voice, "I know he got off the train I saw him walk past the window. Uncle Jim, did you notice an old gentleman wearing a floppy old hat, with long white hair, a long white beard, and a big round tummy?"

"Nope, can't say that I 'ave. I'm the only old man I've seen around here today with a big round tummy, that's for sure."

"But Uncle Jim, he couldn't have just vanished into thin air?"

"I see no reason why not." Said Uncle Jim, lifting his cap and giving his head a scratch.

"Uncle Jim," said Mummy, "you are as bad as your sister

believing in such things."

"Well, May, I only knows what I have seen with my own eyes, then the very next minute not seen — if you get my drift. Your Aunty says I am nothing but a silly old fool, I s'pose I is, most of the time. But don't you worry your pretty little head, young Hetty. You mark my words, in a day or so your Mr Christmas will turn up again right before your very eyes."

"Now come on, or else I will be in trouble, with your Aunty Lily. There is a spread of food back at the cottage fit for a Queen, or did I ought to say Princess. I also knows there is some lovely homemade fruitcake just waiting to be enjoyed, you see little maid, I had my orders it was not to be touched until you arrived, now what do you think about that?"

Uncle Jim loaded the luggage into the car.

"Good job I brought the big car," he said, "this old case only just fits in the boot! You planning on leaving home, Princess?"

Hetty smiled.

"Now that's more like it. We can't have you going around with a long face, you will turn the milk sour. Now jump in, we best be on our way."

"I think you are a very funny, Uncle Jim." Hetty giggled.

"That I be." He said proudly. "Now, May, who is this 'Mr Christmas' anyways?"

"Oh, just an old Gentleman Hetty met at the station before we left. But it does all seem a little strange, don't you think? People don't just vanish do they?"

"Well, that depends." Said Uncle Jim, smiling to himself.

As they arrived at the cottage, Aunty Lily was waiting at the garden gate drying her hands on her apron. She looked so happy to see them.

"It's a hot day today, my dears, now lets get you all inside for some lunch. You must be very hungry. Perhaps later we can go out in the garden to enjoy a cool drink, and a piece of my very best fruitcake."

Sitting around the rickety table under the apple tree, it felt so lovely in the dappled sunlight.

"Goodness me, Jim," said Aunty Lily, "our Hetty certainly knows how to chatter. Now just look how happy old Smudge is to see her again, barking then dashing around like a bee in a tis. I think we are in for a noisy time, don't you my dear?"

Uncle Jim just smiled and nodded while enjoying quite a large slice of delicious cake.

Aunty Lily and Uncle Jim never had children of their own, so they loved to have Hetty or her cousins to stay in their little cottage by the sea.

The very next morning there was a loud knock on the kitchen door.

Hetty ran to open it, there was Beth and Ruth, jumping up and down with excitement.

"Goodness, when did you arrive?" Hetty asked.

"Last night, far too late for us to come over."

"Gosh, we are both so happy to be here again."

"Come in and meet everyone." Hetty smiled.

"Hello, you two," said Mummy, "did your Mummy drive you down?"

"Yes."

"And she has asked if you would like to pop around and join her for a cup of tea."

"I would love to," said Mummy, "I am sure you girls will have a lot to chatter about, so I will see you in a little while."

The next few days were full of holiday fun; walks to the beach, playing in the sea, collecting shells or building sand castles.

The sun shone every day. It really was the most perfect summer holiday...

Dunster Church

Chapter 4

Dunster

It was time for Hetty's Mummy to return home. Uncle Jim drove everyone to the station.

Mummy gave Hetty a huge hug, "Now make sure you brush your hair and clean your teeth."

"I will, Mummy, I promise."

Everyone blew kisses and waved until the train was out of sight.

"Hetty, perhaps you would be so kind later to take Uncle Jim's lunch up to the garage for him? You see he will be very busy this time of the year."

So with Uncle Jim's lunch tucked safely in a basket, Hetty made her way up the steep hill to the village.

"My word, little maid, you look as you are about to melt! It sure is a hot one today. Now I reckon you could do with a nice ice cream to put you right, then you make sure you find a cool place to sit for a while."

"Thank you very much, Uncle Jim."

"Here you are, young lady, you can keep the change — a tip for bringing me my lunch. And very nice it is too." He said as he gave Hetty a few coins. "Please don't look so forlorn, little one, when I gets home I will see if there are some sweet ripe strawberries for tea. Now, that ought to put a smile on your face."

"Thank you, Uncle Jim, that will be really lovely."

Hetty strolled along to the corner shop and bought a large strawberry cone. It tasted perfect. As Beth and Ruth were out for the day, Hetty was feeling a little lost as to what to do. I know, she thought, I think I will visit the dovecote. Hetty loved the beautiful white doves.

Enjoying her ice cream, she wandered slowly up the lane, past the old village school, then through the stone arch just behind the Church. There was the dovecote, a tall round building made from local stone. Inside, lining the walls from top to bottom, were little nesting boxes.

Hetty crept very quietly forward so she could hear the doves cooing. It was such a lovely, happy sound. Then suddenly, without warning, the doves took off, swooping high up into the sky. The swish and flapping from their wings made a cool breeze across Hetty's face.

Up and up they flew, high above the Church. They looked so beautiful swooping around the rooftops, like a huge fluttering white cloud. Then all of a sudden, they returned to the dovecote

Dunster Dovecote

just as quickly as they had left. And the chatter and cooing started over again.

Sitting herself down in the shade, feeling so very hot and tired, she gave a deep sigh then closed her eyes.

"Oh doves beautiful white doves do tell me, will my wishes ever come true? Will I ever meet the fairies? Grandma told me I just have to keep wishing and wishing that's all, then maybe one day…"

Hetty drifted into a gentle sleep. Curiously, the cooing seemed to be getting louder and louder…

"Oh lovely doves what can I do?" She wondered.

"The wishing well. Go to the wishing well," the doves cooed.

"The wishing well! Goodness," gasped Hetty, suddenly leaping to her feet. "Oh thank you, beautiful doves, it has to be the best place in the whole world to make a wish. Why had I not thought of it before?"

Opposite the dovecote, hidden behind a little wooden door is a very pretty walled garden. This is what Hetty called her secret garden, although it really belonged to the church. It is such a magical place, full of sweet smelling flowers, busy bumble bees or happy singing little birds.

But, most importantly, in the garden was a wishing well.

Sitting herself gently down onto the wooden seat against the wall, with the wishing well just in front of her, Hetty paused for moment or two. This might be my only chance for my wishes to come true, she thought to herself. Gazing longingly into the well,

she thought very carefully about what she was going to ask for in her wish.

With the change from her ice cream held firmly in her hand, she stood up very slowly, keeping her eyes tightly closed. Then, taking a deep breath, Hetty made her wish and threw her pennies into the well.

"Oh wishing well, wishing well, please, please make my wishes come true."

Later that evening, Hetty snuggled down in her cosy bed with her beloved teddy bear. I wonder if wishes really do come true, she sighed. Oh well, I will just have to wait and see.

The next day, Hetty met up with Beth and Ruth. They thought, for a change, instead of going to the beach, they would walk to the village to meet up with some of their friends. Everyone agreed to walk to the playing field to enjoy a game of cricket.

Along the way, Hetty asked Tom (one of the boys from the village), if the fast flowing stream at the edge of the lane flowed down to the sea.

"No, Hetty, it flows all the way down to the old watermill on the edge of the Castle woods." Tom replied.

"Heavens, a watermill!" Exclaimed Hetty. "That sounds great fun, can we go and have a look?"

"Not likely," said Tom, "well you can go if you like, but everyone says there is an old witch that lives at the mill and if she catches you messing around she might turn you into a toad."

That sounds very scary, thought Hetty. Even so it was all very intriguing.

"Come on," said Tom, "the others are waiting for us."

Later, Hetty couldn't stop thinking about the old witch and the watermill. Could it be true? She wondered. I really must try to find out more...

It was Saturday, market day. Aunty Lily was placing jars of her homemade jam into a large basket on the kitchen table. Hetty was given the job of putting cotton covers over the lids, (made from blue and white checked gingham held in place with an elastic band), then adding the sticky labels that read 'Homemade Strawberry Jam'.

"Now, young lady, we had best be on our way," said Aunty Lily, "or we will miss finding a table. It all gets very busy at the Market this time of the year."

Off they went, making their way up the steep hill to the village. As they approached the Yarn Market, Hetty could not believe her eyes. For there, chatting to an old lady selling brightly coloured ribbons from baskets all around, was...

MR CHRISTMAS!

"Aunty Lily, look its my Mr Christmas! You know the old gentleman I met at the station? He is just over there talking to an old lady." Hetty exclaimed. "Uncle Jim was right! He said one day he would turn up again and he has, don't you think that's amazing?"

Aunty squinted her eyes against the sun.

"Oh yes, that old lady has been coming here for years. The thing is, young Hetty, she looked just the same when I was your age — goodness knows how old she is now. She keeps herself to herself most of the time, never seems to go out. Only here to sell her ribbons — we can never work out where they come from. You see, there is nowhere around these parts where you can buy such beautiful things. I must say, over the years it has been a bit of a mystery. She has always lived quite alone in the old watermill on the edge of the castle woods."

"Goodness Aunty Lily, Tom said an old witch lived in the old mill, and that if she caught you sneaking around she might turn you into a toad. Do you think it could be true?"

"Well, that has been the story over the years, but I think it is just a load of old tittle tattle if you ask me. That's all it is, I am sure of it. Now I must get a move on, there seems to be have been too much chatter going on today."

Aunty carefully arranged her strawberry jam into neat rows.

"Thank you, Hetty, you have been such a great help."

"Please can I go now Aunty Lily? I really must go over and say hello I wonder if he will remember me."

Hetty slowly walked over to Mr Christmas, then tapped him gently on his arm.

"Excuse me Sir, do you remember me? We met at the station."

"Yes of course, hello again young lady, now let me see. Hetty, I believe."

"Goodness! You remembered my name."

"Oh yes, you see I have to remember the names of all the children. It is a very important part of my job. Now, I do hope are you enjoying your holiday."

"Oh yes, very much thank you. Today I have come to the

market with my Aunty Lily. She has brought along some of her homemade strawberry jam to sell, I have really enjoyed helping her get it all ready."

"Delicious," said Mr Christmas, "it is one off my most favourite things. Maybe I ought to buy a pot of jam for my tea."

"I am sure you will enjoy it, you see it is made from my Uncle Jim's delicious strawberries."

"Even better," said Mr Christmas. "As you have been such a help to your Aunty, I wonder if you would like to have a ribbon for you hair?"

"Thank you, I would love one," said Hetty. "They are all very beautiful, but I think I like the pink ones best of all."

The old lady pulled out a shiny pink ribbon from her basket and handed it to Hetty. She smiled a gentle smile. Hetty thought she looked too kind to really be a witch.

"Thank you very much," said Hetty.

"You are most welcome," whispered the Old lady. "Look after it and make sure you keep it very safe. You see, it is a very special ribbon."

"Oh I will, I promise. It is so beautiful," said Hetty, "the loveliest pink ribbon I have ever seen."

Mr Christmas bought his pot of jam, saying thank you to Aunty Lily.

"I must be off now, lots to do — it all keeps me very busy."

Then suddenly, just as before, he simply vanished right before their eyes!

"Oh my goodness! Now do you believe me?" Laughed Hetty, almost bursting with excitement.

Poor Aunty Lily looked more than a little flustered. Quickly smoothing down her apron, she then set about rearranging her jars into neat rows.

"I am sure it was just a trick of the light. Even so, it did seem very strange and quite unexplainable. Such peculiar goings on. All in all it has made me feel quite dizzy." She said, quickly sitting herself down while mopping her brow with a tea towel, "what a carry on it all is, I must say."

All Hetty could do was giggle, "That was amazing, don't you think?"

"Aunty Lily, I must go and tell Uncle Jim what has happened — this is so exciting."

"Yes go on then, off you go, but I really must stay here."

Hetty arrived at the garage calling out "Uncle Jim, Uncle Jim, where are you?" Uncle Jim came out from the workshop wiping his hands on an oily old cloth.

"Is everything all right, little one? Where's your Aunty Lily?"

"Don't worry, Uncle Jim, she is still at the Yarn Market selling her jam." Hetty smiled. "Uncle Jim, you were quite right! Guess who was there talking to the Old lady selling her beautiful ribbons, it was my Mr Christmas."

"Well bless my soul, such excitement! Then what happened?"

"Well," said Hetty, "do you know he actually remembered my

name, then he kindly bought me this lovely pink ribbon for my hair, and a pot of Aunty's strawberry jam. Then oh my goodness! Guess what happened next?"

"Well," said Uncle Jim, "I'm listening."

"After a few moments, Mr Christmas just vanished again right before our very eyes!"

"Now that would have unnerved your Aunty Lily, that's for sure."

"She did look a little surprised also very flustered," giggled Hetty.

"Well what a day it has turned out to be," said Uncle Jim, "I wonder what will happen next?"

Later that evening, Hetty held up her lovely pink ribbon. It twinkled and shimmered in the gentle evening light. It felt so soft and silky as she gently held it against her face.

She thought about the old lady and the watermill. I wonder, could she really be a witch? I just have to find out more. Why was she talking to my Mr Christmas? And where do all the beautiful ribbons come from? Goodness, I must go to the mill as soon as I can. I just hope I don't get turned into a toad.

Hetty sighed as she tucked the ribbon carefully under her pillow. Soon she was fast asleep...

Chapter 5

Out for a walk

It was Sunday morning. The sound of church bells drifted down across the village. Hetty welcomed the smell of toast and bacon drifting up from the kitchen, quickly she made her way down the funny old twisted staircase.

"Good morning, little one," said Uncle Jim, "I hope you are feeling hungry. Your Aunty Lily says she needs to fatten you up. She reckons there is more fat on a ferret than on your ribs, must be all the running around you've been doing. Mind you, your Mummy was just the same at your age — not enough fat on her either to keep a poacher happy, that's for sure."

"It's a pity you don't do a bit more running around yourself, Jim Parsons," said Aunty Lily, "that old tummy of yours is getting bigger and rounder every day."

"Ah now, that be a sign of a happy man, my dear."

"That's as may be, but a little less butter on your toast won't go amiss." Aunty Lily replied smiling.

"Hetty, don't she keep on nagging me? Going on something rotten so in the end I just gives in! Anything to keep the peace."

Hetty giggled and patted his big round tummy.

"Honestly, you two are just as bad as each other." Said Aunty Lily.

"So what are you going to be up to today, little maid?"

"I am not really sure, you see, Beth and Ruth are going over to Minehead for the day. Tom did say he might call in for me and we might go for a walk up through the woods to Conygar Tower."

"Well, I must say 'tis a very long time since I have been up to the Tower," said Uncle Jim, "many a time I walked up there with your Aunty Lily when we was doing a bit of courting — we used to take a picnic and all. But it must have gotten a bit overgrown by now, I would think. Ah, that were a few years ago, my dear, can you remember me wooing you? Your Aunty Lily was the prettiest girl in the village, made me proper proud to have her on my arm."

"Oh for goodness sake, Jim Parsons, you are making me blush! Now finish your toast and get out from under my feet. I have never heard such a load of old nonsense." Aunty Lily said, though she couldn't quite hide her smile.

Uncle Jim got up from the table then gave Aunty Lily a big squeeze and peck on the cheek.

"You silly old thing, now look what you have made me do," as an egg went splat onto the kitchen floor.

"Oh well, never mind," said Uncle Jim, "old Smudge will enjoy it for his breakfast."

"Honest to goodness, Hetty, your Uncle is getting much worse as he gets older." Aunty Lily sighed. "Now, for goodness sake go out into the garden and do something useful so I can clear up this floor. What a morning it is turning out to be! Your Uncle Jim loves working in his garden, just like your Daddy, Hetty."

"Yes that's right," Hetty replied, "I sometimes I like to help in the garden, but you see he loves his rose garden most of all. Do you know Daddy always picks the first summer rose for Mummy, wraps the stem in silver paper then as he hands it to her he gives her a little kiss and tells her how much he loves her."

"I think that is very romantic, don't you?" Aunty Lily nodded.

"Aunty Lily, is Uncle Jim romantic?"

"Well, I don't know about romantic. He always makes sure he wipes his feet when he comes in, then thanks me when I cooks him a nice tea. Oh yes, he always brings me home a lovely Christmas tree on Christmas Eve. So that is kind of romantic, don't you think? And on my birthday he buys me a nice box of chocolates, but mind you, my dear Hetty, I am sure he eats most of them himself. You see he always says 'you can never eat diamonds'. Really, your silly old Uncle Jim seems to have an answer for everything Now I must get on and clear up this kitchen, goodness me I have never seen it in such a mess!"

Smudge was suddenly startled from his slumber by a loud knock on the kitchen door. He barked, sending him bouncing around the kitchen.

"Come in!" Called out Aunty Lily.

The door opened and there was Tom with a huge smile showing off his newly fitted braces and looking very excited.

"It is very nice to see you, Tom," said Aunty Lily. "My word, you're getting proper tall, and turning into a very handsome young man too, I must say."

"Thank you." Said Tom, looking just a little self-conscious.

"I can see your teeth are being fixed, now that is a good thing don't you think? Never had braces like that in my day. Now, what can we do for you?"

"Hetty, Rosie and I are on our way up to Conygar Tower and we wondered if you would like to come with us, if that is alright with your Aunty?"

"That will be fine," said Aunty Lily, "but make sure you all keep together. We don't want any of you getting lost in them woods. But first, put this noisy dog out into the garden. I must say, it's all been a bit of a rumpus here this morning."

"Sorry," said Tom, "perhaps we could take Smudge out for a walk later?"

"That would be wonderful, my dears, at last I will be able to enjoy a bit of peace and quiet. Now off you go and let me get on with cleaning this kitchen floor."

Tom, Hetty and Rosie felt as if they were going on a bit of an adventure as they entered the Tower woods, rambling happily along making their way up the steep winding path. In places, the path had become so overgrown they had to push and squeeze their way past the dense bushes and ferns.

Stopping for a moment to catch their breath, the wood suddenly fell silent. Not a sound could be heard, except for the trees creaking, rustling and swaying, casting eerie shadows all around.

Hetty started to feel cold and more than a little frightened.

"I don't like it here," said Rosie, "it's dark and very creepy."

"Don't worry," said Tom, "it's quite safe. Listen, I can hear the rooks in the distance squawking high up in the tower. Come on, you two, keep up."

At last, they reached the clearing at the top of the hill. Conygar Tower stood before them, many of its walls were covered in thick green moss. Exchanging nervous glances, Rosie held on to Hetty's hand as they crept slowly, slowly forward.

"Wow," said Tom, "it's enormous!"

High overhead, they could see the huge black rooks swooping and swirling around the tree tops. Their horrid feathers were black, black as the darkest night.

"I don't like rooks," said Rosie, "I am sure witches have rooks in their caverns."

"Oh don't," whispered Hetty, "now you are making me feel really scared."

"Rooks won't hurt you," said Tom, "they just squawk a lot. You are just being silly girls. Now come on, let's have a game of hide and seek. But first we must try to find the entrance to a secret tunnel."

"A tunnel?" The girls exclaimed, glancing nervously at each other.

"Yes," said Tom, "apparently there is a tunnel that goes from the tower all the way over to the castle."

"Now that's making me feel even more frightened," said Hetty.

"I think I want to go back now," said Rosie, "it's cold and dark in here, and sometimes truly horrid things live in woods, don't they Hetty?"

"Don't you want to play hide and seek? There are loads of places to hide."

"No, thank you, we just want to go back."

"You two are nothing but a pair of scaredy girls," said Tom.

Even so, they all ran as fast as they could back down the twisting path, passing through the thick ferns bushes and rustling trees, until at last they burst out into the warm sunshine. Throwing themselves down onto a grassy bank.

Gasping for breath, Hetty gave a shiver. It was good to feel warm and safe again. After feeling so frightened, she thought she would leave going down to the old watermill for another day.

Turning onto their backs they gazed up at the sky.

"Rosie and Tom, can I ask you both a question?"

"Of course," said Tom, "as long as it's not silly girls stuff."

"Well, I have been wondering," said Hetty, "do you think people or things could simply vanish right before your eyes?"

"Heavens," said Tom. "I have never thought about that before. Well, what sort of things?"

"I don't know," said Hetty.

"Well now, let me think," said Tom, "magicians make things disappear."

"No, that's not what I mean," said Hetty, "that's just a magic show."

Suddenly, Rosie leapt to her feet and in a very loud voice shouted out, "Rainbows disappear, don't they?"

"Yes, Rosie, you are quite right!" Exclaimed Tom. "One minute there is a gleaming arch of colours right across the sky, then it all slowly just fades away as if it was never there."

"That's like real magic," said Rosie.

Yes, thought Hetty, real magic.

After lunch, they all met up to take Smudge out for his walk. He pulled on his lead and sniffed at everything.

"He is making my arms hurt," said Hetty.

"Give him to me," said Tom, "I am much stronger than you."

"I think he knows he is going to the beach," giggled Rosie, "just look how fast his tail is waggling."

"Listen!" Exclaimed Hetty. "I can hear the train in the distance. Quickly, if we run to the level crossing we can climb on the gate and wave as it goes past."

The children arrived just in time to see the huge black steam train rumbling towards them. The train track creaked under the enormous weight of the engine, so huge and powerful. It towered over them engulfing the children in an explosion of sound. The piercing noise from the whistle made the girls leap down from the gate, clasping their hands over their ears. The blast of steam suddenly swept over them. Billowing smoke from the chimney was sent soaring upwards, leaving huge white waves across the blue sky. The ground gently trembled beneath their feet.

Heavy carriages followed, full of happy waving children on their way to the seaside. Then all in a blur, it was gone.

"Phew! How cool was that?" Said Tom, as the lane fell silent once again.

All except for poor Smudge who was shaking and whining.

Tom gave him a hug.

"Don't worry, old thing, when the gates open up we can run to the beach, I am sure you will soon forget all about the horrid noisy train."

The train made Hetty think about her Mr Christmas. I wonder if I will ever meet him again, she sighed.

The old gentleman who lived at Railway Cottage came out to join them.

"Afternoon children, I'd best open up the gates to let you through. I see you are taking old Smudge out for a walk. Now, I already knows young Tom and Rosie, so you must be Hetty. I have heard all about you coming to stay."

"Yes that's right, I am staying with my Aunty Lily and Uncle Jim for two weeks. Can I ask, how do you know Smudge?"

"Ah well, you see that old Jim Parsons is an old mate of mine. I can remember when he gave the puppy to Lily one Christmas, many moons ago now, so he must be getting a bit long in the tooth like the rest of us. Jim would give her the world if he could.

You see, underneath he is just a proper soft old so and so. Now that's enough of me nattering, I'd best be getting on. I'm just about to pick some lovely runner beans — as sweet as honey they are, and far more than I need. So I will leave some by my kitchen door, you can pick them up on your way back from the beach. Then later, Lily can cook them for your tea with an egg and new tatties. Nothing better than that, just lovely."

"Thank you very much," said Hetty, "that is very kind of you."

"That's all right, my dear," he said, giving them toothless grin. "You see, I am a canny old thing, and with any luck your Uncle Jim will pay me back with a few of his prize winning strawberries. Now that can't be a bad thing, don't you think? There now, you youngsters, the gates are open and you can be on your way. Good day to you."

He gave the children a wicked wink as he made his way down the cottage path, chuckling away to himself.

The children made one last stop before they reached the beach, they went to say hello to Old Tim. Old Tim was quite a character. He had lived for many years in his little home at the side of the lane. He built it himself from stones, pebbles and shells he collected from the beach. He often wore a white pith helmet and would stand and salute as people passed his little home by the sea.

Hetty, Rosie and Tom waved and said goodbye to Old Tim, running off down to the beach. Smudge led the way, with his tail wagging happily once more.

Chapter 6
The watermill

"Goodness, when is this hot weather ever going to end?" Sighed Aunty Lily. "It hasn't been this warm for years — it's far too hot for cooking, that's for sure. You seem in a bit of a daze this morning little maid."

"Not really," Hetty sighed, "I was just wondering if I am ever going see my Mr Christmas again, that's all."

"Well," said Aunty Lily, "my mother always use to say: 'what will be, will be and that you can never alter, you will just have to wait and see'. One thing's for sure, you're not going to see him sitting around here all day with a long face."

"But Aunty Lily, you did meet my Mr Christmas and he did just disappear right before your eyes."

"That's as may be, but you know I don't believe in all these sorts of things. I have enough of your Uncle Jim telling me what he has seen over the years, then not seen."

"But you have to believe in fairies, Aunty Lily! Granny told me that she believes so, that is good enough for me. I will just have to keep wishing and wishing that's all."

Hetty suddenly thought about the watermill. "Goodness! I have just remembered something."

"That's more like it young lady, now off you go and make sure you keep out of mischief."

"I will, I promise," Hetty answered as she went dashing out through the kitchen door, leaving Aunty Lily shaking her head in amusement.

"Children." Aunty Lily muttered to herself. "What a carry on it all is — what with fairies, and Hetty's 'Mr Christmas'. All these comings and goings, I have never heard the likes of it. I think I need to sit down and have a nice quiet cup of tea."

Hetty dashed next door to ask if the twins would like to go to the mill.

Beth opened the door with a very long face.

"Mum said we have to stay in this morning and wash our hair, but we could meet you after lunch?"

"Goodness Hetty, why are you in such a rush?" Ruth asked, seeing Hetty's disappointment.

"I will have to tell you later, but I must go now and see if I can find Tom. See you this afternoon at the playing field by the stream," called Hetty as she ran back up the garden path, "bring along the cricket bats and balls!"

Hetty found Tom chatting with his friends.

"Oh Tom, please come with me it's very, very important. I just have to go and find out more."

"Goodness Hetty, what ever has happened?"

"It's the mill, Tom. I have to go to the mill and if you don't come with me I will go on my own. But at least if I tell you and I don't come back, you will know I have been turned into a toad."

"Now calm down Het, there's no need to rush. The watermill has been standing there for hundreds of years." Tom sighed. "All right, I will come with you. But first, you had better ask your Aunty Lily if we can go up to the village."

"I will," Hetty called out as she ran back down the lane.

She burst through the kitchen door, almost making Aunty Lily drop her cup of tea.

"For goodness sake Hetty, what in heavens name is going on this time? You gave me quite a fright."

"I'm so sorry Aunty, but I just wanted ask if I could go up to the village with Tom?"

"You are not going anywhere, young lady, until you calm down. Rushing around in this heat is no good to anyone, whatever it is can wait a moment. Now, sit yourself down and have a nice cool drink. I think it would be good thing if you tied your hair back off of your face. Now why don't you go and fetch the pink ribbon the old lady gave you? If you ask me, that will do the job very nicely."

Hetty leapt to her feet, "Aunty Lily you are a genius! Goodness why didn't I think of that?"

She gave Aunty Lilly a huge hug, before dashing up the rickety stairs to her bedroom. Reaching under pillow she carefully pulled out her beautiful pink ribbon. Sitting down at the dressing table, Hetty brushed the tangles from her hair then carefully slipped the ribbon under the back of her hair, holding the ends up over her forehead. She paused for a moment, trying to remember how to tie a bow.

Suddenly, to her utter amazement, the ribbon quickly unwound from her fingers and tied itself into a perfect bow on the top of her head.

"Oh my goodness," she gasped as she stared in astonishment, "it's a magic ribbon!"

Then, taking a second look into the mirror, the ribbon twinkled in her reflection.

"Heavens, I wonder what will happen next?"

When Hetty entered the kitchen, Aunty Lily could not believe her eyes. Could it really be Hetty standing there with her hair looking as pretty as a picture?

"Well my maid, you be looking like a proper young lady, not like a tomboy anymore. Bless my soul never thought I would see the day."

"Please can I go now?" Hetty asked, almost bursting with excitement.

"Yes, go on then," said Aunty Lily, "here now, take a couple of apples with you for later. Our best crop ever — lovely and sweet they are.

"Thank you," said Hetty, quickly stuffing the two apples into her dress pockets.

Tom was whistling to himself as he ambled down the lane. Hetty ran to meet him.

"You look nice," he said, "you look as though you are going to a party. Gosh, it is a very sparkly ribbon."

"Yes it is," agreed Hetty, "and very special too. You see, Tom, I think I will have to tell you the whole story, but only if you promise to keep it a secret.

"I promise," said Tom, "cross my heart."

They made their way up to the village, then as they slowly walked down the lane towards the watermill, Hetty began to tell Tom her magic story.

She explained her very first meeting with Mr Christmas, at the station while she was waiting for her train. Then later, when they had arrived at Dunster and Hetty had seen Mr Christmas dash pass the window of the train but then vanish into thin air.

"Uncle Jim thought this was nothing unusual. Tom, don't you think that was a very strange thing for him to say? People don't just vanish, do they?"

"Goodness Hetty, that does sound very mysterious. What happened next?"

"Well, on another day, I went for a walk to visit to the dovecote.

It was a very hot day, Uncle Jim gave me some money to buy an ice cream then told me to find a cool place to sit for a while. As I was sitting in the cool shade of the dovecote I started to feel very sleepy. But then an amazing thing happened, the lovely white doves spoke to me. They told me I must to go to the wishing well and make a wish."

Hetty sighed and smiled as she remembered it all.

"Oh Tom, was I dreaming or did it really happen? Then, next market day, I helped Aunty Lily take her jams up to the village. When we arrived at the yarn market, I could not believe my eyes, for there was my Mr Christmas talking to the Old Lady who lives in the watermill on the edge of the castle woods!

"Mr Christmas bought a pot of strawberry jam, then the old lady let me choose my pink ribbon. But you see, Tom, it's not just a lovely pink sparkly ribbon, it truly is a very magic ribbon."

"Heavens Hetty, no wonder you want to find out more." Tom said.

Suddenly, they both stopped in their tracks as the watermill came into view.

"You see Tom, that's why I am wearing my pink ribbon. I do hope the old lady will remember me and not turn us both into toads."

"Well, we will soon find out."

Creeping slowly and quietly towards the huge oak door, Hetty reached out for Tom's hand and held it very tightly.

But before they had time to knock, the door flew open and there stood the old lady dressed in long black clothes, with her long grey hair, and her long crooked nose.

"Good morning, my dears, how can I help you?" She asked.

Hetty was rooted to the spot, unable to say a word.

"Good morning," said Tom in a very shaky voice, "we just thought it would be nice to come and pay you a visit."

"Well then, my dears, you had better come in."

Both children glanced nervously at each other.

"I am just about to make some lovely herbal tea, would you like some refreshment? Perhaps a cool drink would be nice."

"No, thank you." They both said shaking their heads, fearing it might be poison.

The old lady left to make her tea. This gave the children a moment to look around. It was nice and cool inside. There were lots of cobwebs hanging about, but apart from that, there was no sign of a crystal ball, or a black rook, not even a witch's broom. In fact, it all seemed quite cosy.

Hetty finally let go Toms hand.

"What do you think?" He asked.

But before Hetty had time to answer, the old lady returned. She sat herself down in a large wooden rocking chair placing her green herbal tea onto a small round table. Both children stared in horror at the swirling liquid thinking it must surely be Witch's Brew.

"I hope you like your ribbon, Hetty." She said. "I must say, pink suits you very well."

"Goodness, you remembered my name!" Hetty gasped.

"I never forget a name, my dear. As you may have already discovered, it is a very special magic ribbon, only given to those who we can truly trust."

Hetty nodded her head and smiled, even though she felt more than a little confused.

At this point, Tom could not hold back any longer.

"Can you really turn children into toads?" He asked.

"What do you think, Tom? Do you think it might be true?" The old lady replied.

"Gosh, you know my name. How do you do that?"

"It is just a gift that has been given to me, no more than that. As for turning children into toads, it's a tale that has been told around here for many years. You see, if it keeps children away from the mill, or the secret of the castle woods, I am very happy to be called a witch. I must say, as I have become very old now, I think I make a very good witch don't you?"

"Oh yes," giggled Hetty, "you did make us a little scared."

"What is the rumbling sound?" asked Tom.

"It's the mill working," the old lady replied. "I am milling some flour for my friends."

"Goodness, do you really have friends?" Hetty asked. "Only,

everyone seems to think you live here all alone."

"That is true, but I do have lots of little friends. You see, they don't have money like you, so I mill them some flour and they repay me with the most beautiful ribbons in all the colours of a rainbow. That is as much as I am going to say. Now, Hetty and Tom, it must remain our secret, do you understand?"

"Yes we promise," said the children, "cross our hearts."

"Thank you both for coming, but I must get back to the mill. My little friends will soon need the flour to make cakes for their tea."

Tom and Hetty said their goodbyes to the old lady. They stopped just outside the mill to take a look through the tall metal gates at the path leading up to the Castle woods. All they could see in the distance was a stone bridge over the stream, there was the soft sound of the babbling brook and birds chattering in the trees.

"Well," said Tom, "it looks just like a normal wood to me. And as the gates are firmly locked, this is as far as we can go. I am very thirsty and hungry, I wish we had had that drink now."

Hetty remembered the apples in her pockets and gave one to Tom.

"Oh thanks, Het, this will do the trick."

Eating their apples, they slowly made their way back up the lane. Hetty was feeling very sad and forlorn.

The old lady was not a witch after all. Although, she did seem to have some strange powers. It was all so very disappointing.

"What would you like to do now, Hetty?"

"Well," she sighed, "first I would like to paddle my feet in the stream and have a little rest. I am feeling very hot and tired. Then we can make our way back to the playing field. Before we left, I asked Beth to meet us there and bring along the cricket bat and balls."

"Oh great," said Tom, "I will go and see if a few of my friends would like to join us."

"That would be good," Hetty sighed.

"Don't sound so disappointed, Het. You will see your Mr Christmas again, I am sure of it. Now try and cheer yourself up."

They reached the stream. Hetty slipped off her sandals, sitting herself down on the shady bank, gently lowering her feet into the water. It felt refreshingly cool as it as it ran between her toes.

"See you later then," said Tom as he set off to find his friends.

It felt lovely to have a moment to herself. Closing her eyes, Hetty enjoyed listening to the stream as it trickled gently over the stones.

But there was another sound.

Straining her ears, Hetty was sure she could hear someone crying.

"Hello?" She whispered. "Is anyone there? I can hear you but I can't see you."

"I am over here," said a tiny little voice.

Hetty was spellbound. For there, sitting on a lily pad was a beautiful little fairy.

"Oh goodness, there you are!" Hetty blinked, feeling as if her heart would stop beating with excitement. "Why are you crying?"

"My wings are all wet and I am not able to fly," the fairy sobbed.

Before Hetty could say another word, a large green frog wearing a golden crown leapt out from the hedgerow. Hetty was rooted to the spot. She rubbed her eyes and looked back again in utter amazement.

"Dear me," said the frog, "goodness, it's new fairy season again. Fairies must remember they are fairies. Leaping around on the lily pads is for us frogs. This happens every year, my dear, it's a jolly good job I keep a good eye on things around here." He turned to Hetty very seriously. "You see, they get their wings all wet and then can't fly home. I would dearly love to put up a very large sign to announce that fairies are not allowed on the lily pads. But that would cause no end of trouble — people would read it too, and I have enough to do without children tramping through the woods trying to find the fairies. That would be the most frightful nuisance. Now then, I had better get on with the job in hand and see about getting this little fairy safely home."

The frog was wearing a brown bag over his shoulder, and a whistle around his neck. He took this and blew it three times. After a moment, a large grey rabbit leapt out from the bushes.

Hetty was speechless.

"Good afternoon, Bertie. Now then, my good fellow, I have a job for you. If you would be so kind as to run this little fairy home? You see, she has managed to get her wings wet and is not able to fly."

"Not a problem," said the rabbit, "I will do it right away."

"Hooray, splendid, awfully good of you," said the frog.

"All in a days work," answered the rabbit, "very glad to help."

"Now just hold on a tick," the frog pulled the lily pad over to the bank and the little fairy climbed onto the rabbit's back, snuggling herself down into his warm fur.

"Not to worry, your wings will soon be dry." Said the frog. "Make sure you take it steady, Bertie, we don't want her falling off. She's had enough of a fright for one day."

The little fairy gave Hetty a teary smile.

"Now wait for just a moment before you go, I will need to write up my accident report." Said the frog. "Little fairy, please do tell me your name."

"My name is Fern," she answered, "and I am very sorry to have caused so much trouble."

"Not to worry," said the frog, "it's all part of growing up. Just remember in future to stay away from water, flying is what you do best — not swimming! Bertie will soon have you safely home and, with any luck, just in time for your delicious tea."

"I will be off now then," said the rabbit.

"Thank you, Bertie, you really are jolly good sport, without doubt a very great help to me for getting a most satisfying job done."

The frog turned to Hetty.

"Well, you seem a very nice young lady." He said. "I don't think I have seen you here before. But I believe your name to be Hetty, quite a charming name for a young lady, I must say."

All Hetty could do was nod her head. Her mouth was far too dry to say anything.

"Now let me introduce myself. I am Henry, King of the Frogs. As you can see, I like to run a very tight ship. I always make sure I keep a keen eye on things around the castle and, of course, the castle woods. The tower woods, on the other hand, are looked after by King Rook. He really is the most loathsome creature, repeatedly making trouble for everyone. If you listen, you can hear the rooks squawking, all the way up in their tower. They really are a most noisy and tiresome bunch." King Frog sighed. "Well my dear, it has been quite a splendid day, thankfully with a very happy ending. Now I must be off to enjoy my tea. Good day to you, my dear Hetty…"

Quite suddenly he was gone.

"King Frog," whispered Hetty, "please can I visit you again?"

Hetty was so happy. At last, she had met a beautiful little fairy.

Thank you, doves, my wish has come true. Granny was right after all, there are fairies that live in the woods.

"Where were you, Hetty?" Beth called. "We have been waiting for you for ages. Goodness, you look very dazed. What is the matter? You look as if you have seen a ghost!"

"I think I may have fallen asleep…"

Or did I? Hetty wondered.

"Oh Beth, I dreamt that I met the sweetest little fairy called Fern, a talking frog, and a large grey rabbit called Bertie, who seems to run the most excellent fairy taxi service."

"Heavens," said Beth, "I think you must have had too much sun. Now Hetty, you must remember to wear a sun hat tomorrow."

"Don't worry Beth, I am fine. Perfectly fine. I have never been happier," Hetty giggled. "But I must rush home right away, and write a very important letter to my Grandma. I am sure she will love to hear my most amazing news."

"Hetty, are you sure you are feeling well?" Beth asked.

"Oh yes, I have never felt better," Hetty called out as she went dashing up the lane.

Goodness, thought Beth, I wonder what has happened for Hetty to be so excited?

Chapter 7
Through the gates

Hetty came charging through the kitchen door.

"Hetty I wish you would stop doing that, you nearly made me drop my cup of tea! My goodness, just look at how hot you are again."

"Yes I know, Aunty Lily, I ran all the way home. I must find Uncle Jim, do you know where he is? He is not at the garage — all the doors are locked, and the closed sign was out in the yard."

"He is out in the back garden digging up some tatties for our tea, what in heavens name is it this time?"

"It's the fairies, Aunty Lily, at last I have actually met a real little fairy, a talking frog and a rabbit running a taxi service. Don't you think it is wonderful? Just truly very, very funny."

"What did I tell you? I knew it was too hot for you to go dashing about in this heat, now sit yourself down and have a nice cool drink."

But it was too late. Hetty was already out through the back door, leaving Aunty Lily shaking her head.

"'Fairies, talking frogs, and a rabbit running a taxi service'. I have never heard the likes of it, everyone around here seems to be going quite mad. It must be the heat doing funny things to people. The sooner it cools down, the better. Now, where did I put my cup of tea?"

"Uncle Jim, Uncle Jim," Hetty called.

"I am over here," he answered. He was sitting under the apple tree. "Goodness me, you look as though you are about to burst with excitement. Whatever it is, you had better sit down beside me and tell me all about it."

Hetty quickly sat herself down and blurted out the whole story, hardly able to get the words out fast enough.

"Well, little maid, what a day you have had. I see you are wearing your pink ribbon, now I think that may have had something to do with it, don't you?"

"That's right, it's a magic ribbon. Did you know that this whole time?"

"Oh yes, you see your Grandma had one just like it when she was a little girl, so I knew it was only a matter of time before magic things would start to happen."

"Oh my goodness, Uncle Jim, isn't it wonderful? Granny has always told me she believed in fairies and now I know why. I must write a letter to her right away and tell her my news. You see, Granny did say if I kept on wishing and wishing long enough, my wishes one day might just come true. And now they have, I have actually met a real little fairy, don't you think it's just so amazing?"

"Yes, truly amazing," chuckled Uncle Jim. "Now, time is getting on so you had best get a move on. I think I had best pop you down in the car to the post box after such a day, I don't want you missing the last collection. Go on, maid, don't just stand there, that letter's sure not going to write itself."

"Oh thank you, Uncle Jim, I do love you. You really are the best Uncle in the whole world."

Hetty went dashing back to the cottage, then up the rickety stairs to her bedroom. Carefully taking her pink ribbon from her hair, she placed it gently under her pillow then quietly whispered;

"Thank you, magic ribbon, thank you for everything. It has been such a magical day."

Uncle Jim slowly wandered back to the kitchen, sitting himself down in his old wooden chair smiling away to himself.

"Well, I must say you look pleased with yourself, Jim Parsons, sitting there with a big sloppy grin on your face."

"Well, it's our young Hetty, Lily, you see she has just said she loves me."

"Of course she does, and so do I, you daft old thing. But that could soon change, mind you, I see you have come in here without the tatties. Now please get a move on or I will never get our tea on the table."

"Oh yes, sorry, I will go and get them right away, then I am going to take her ladyship to the post box. She's upstairs writing a letter to her Grandma."

"You two are as thick as thieves — fairies, letters, dashing about, not to mention her Mr Christmas. I must say, Jim, he did make me come over all funny peculiar at the market, just disappearing like that in a flash. I have never seen the likes of it, the whole place is going quite mad. All in all, it has all it has made me feel quite exhausted, I think I might need to sit down. What a carry on it all is, I must say."

Hetty quickly scribbled down her letter as fast as she could.

"Thank you, Granny. I think you knew all the time that my wishes might come true. Now they have, I am so happy it is all just so exciting. I will tell you more when I get home. I love you loads."

Then, after adding kisses all over the page, she put the letter in the envelope and popped on a stamp.

"Right, all done. Time to go."

Uncle Jim was waiting for her in the kitchen.

"Come on, young lady, we must be on our way."

Hetty jumped into the car beside him.

"Uncle Jim, can I ask you something? Do you think Granny really did meet the fairies when she was a little girl?"

"Oh yes," he said, "she saw them alright, I know that for a fact. You see young Hetty, I was with her on that magic day in the

Castle woods. We met your Mr Christmas too, now what do you think of that?"

"Heavens, Uncle Jim, don't you think it is all quite wonderful?"

"Yes, young Hetty, it was a truly wonderful a day, a day I will never forget. Now hurry up, I see Ed the postman is already here to collect the mail."

Hetty ran over, quickly popping her letter into the post box.

"Phew, that was close!"

"It sure was," said Ed the postman, "it's good job I am running a bit late. I reckon it must be your lucky day, young lady."

"Oh yes, it has been a very lucky day. A truly magical day too."

"Well little one," said Uncle Jim. "I would love to be there when your Grandma reads your news. It will bring back so many happy memories of such a magical time when she was a little girl just like you, my dear Hetty. Now I think it must be time for tea, don't you?"

Hetty could not stop thinking about King frog, little fairy Fern, not forgetting Bertie the Rabbit with his fairy taxi service.

Did I fall asleep? She wondered. Maybe it was all just a dream after all. Oh goodness, I wish Granny could be here. She would know what to do. Hetty thought for a moment. "No time like the present" Granny had always told her, "never put things off until tomorrow that what you can finish today".

That's it, thought Hetty, I must go back to the stream to try to find out more. Carefully placing her magic pink ribbon into her pocket, Hetty crept slowly and quietly down the stairs. She slipped out through the kitchen door, closing it very gently behind her.

Quickly making her way up to the village, she stopped for a moment at the Yarn market, thinking about the last time she was there with Aunty Lily on market day. Hetty sighed as she gazed up at the Castle sitting high up on the hill. I wonder what secrets you might be hiding in your Castle woods, she thought. She moved on past the church, Uncle Jim's garage, the corner shop that most definitely sold the best ice creams in the whole world. Hetty found it difficult to walk quickly on the cobbled pavements as she passed by the charming old cottages with their lovely thatch roofs, pretty window boxes now bursting with beautiful bright summer flowers. On past the gift shops, teashop, village pub, and the old stable yard.

At last, she arrived at the lane leading down to the watermill.

Pausing for a moment, she dipped her hands into the stream and splashed the cool refreshing water onto her face. Then, reaching deep into her pocket, she pulled out her magic pink ribbon and tied it into her hair.

"Oh please, pink ribbon, please make more magic happen today."

Hetty meandered aimlessly down the lane, thinking happily that no one had spotted her, not at all as scared as she was the last time when she was here with Tom. For now she knew the old lady who lived in the mill was not a witch after all.

The lane was so lovely. Hetty enjoyed strolling along in the shade of the trees, she smiled as a bright colourful butterfly fluttered past on the soft warm summer breeze. It really was the most beautiful, perfect summers day.

Hetty took a moment to remember the place where she had met King Frog. Once she had found the place, she sat down on the grassy bank crossing her fingers for good luck. Then, leaning gently forward, she quietly whispered;

"King Frog, it is me — Hetty. I hope you can hear me."

For a moment there was silence, and then…

Suddenly leaping out from behind the ferns, King Frog stood before her. His golden crown glinted in the bright summer sunshine.

"Good day to you, young lady." He said. "I must say, what an extraordinarily fine day it is too, perfectly wonderful in every way, don't you think?"

"If you don't mind me saying, Mr Frog — Oh sorry, I mean, King Frog, you do speak in a very posh way."

"Well I do think it is most important to keep up extremely high standards around here, after we do all live in the Castle grounds. That's not a thing to be sniffed at. Like little fairy Fern, who thought being a frog might be fun, I too have my aspirations." King Frog stood up very tall, while clearing his throat with an extremely polite cough. "You see my dear, I have always rather fancied myself as a Butler."

"Goodness, I am sure you would make the most amazing and wonderful Butler," agreed Hetty.

"I am quite sure that would be the case," said the frog, "but a frog I am. No ordinary frog, mind you, I am King Frog. Therefore, it is my duty to look after the magnificent Castle, and more importantly the secrets hidden deep in the Castle woods. A most splendid position for a frog of my standing, don't you think? In accordance to this, I feel it is extremely important at all times to keep a good account of oneself."

"That does seem like a very important job to me," said Hetty, "after all, I am quite sure little fairy Fern was very happy that you look after things so well."

"Yes, I do feel I do a rather fine job, even though I say it myself." The frog agreed, his chest puffing up with pride. "Even so, young lady, I am quite sure you will be very pleasantly surprised to receive this most important and quite splendid invitation."

Hetty sat spellbound, watching as King Frog reached into his little brown bag and pulled out a note. Once more, he stood to attention and gave another polite cough before he announced...

"I must bring this to your notice, my dear. Now I am quite sure you will be pleasantly surprised to receive this quite remarkable invitation. Unmistakably a great honour, I must say."

"Please King Frog, please tell me more. what does it say?"

"Oh yes," said the frog. "Well my dear Hetty, you have been invited to have tea with the fairies this very day. Quite wonderful, don't you think? Now all your wishes are about to come true."

"Thank you so much!" Giggled Hetty. "Tea with the fairies, it feels like I must be dreaming again."

"Now, we must leave right away," said the frog, "this is all very exciting. This way, follow me, look sharp, keep up, we don't want to be late."

"I just love a wonderful yummy tea, don't you?"

"I must say, it is one of my most favourite things, most enjoyable indeed."

King Frog marched off down the lane towards the watermill with Hetty skipping along beside him. Suddenly, King Frog started to sing a little song:

> We are off to a woodland dale
> Where under the trees
> The pixies dwell
> A fantasy world
> For you to see
> With fairies, magic
> And honey bees.

As they arrived at the mill, the old lady came out to greet them.

"Well, dear Hetty, I see you have received your invitation."

"Oh yes, I am so excited! It all feels like a magic dream."

"No, little one, you are not dreaming. Your wishes are about to come true, you are now going to meet my beautiful little woodland friends." The old lady smiled. "Now off you go, please don't worry, you will be quite safe. As soon as you enter the gates, time will stand still, so you will not be late home. I will wait for you here, then you can tell me all about it when you return."

"Thank you so much," said Hetty. "I never thought this day

would come. Goodness, at last I am going to visit Fairyland."

King Frog and Hetty waited at the tall gates, then after a moment, quite unexplainably, the gates unlocked themselves. They creaked loudly as they slowly, slowly opened.

"Splendid," said the Frog. "Come Hetty, we need to get a move on."

Hetty glanced back at the old lady as the gates slowly closed, magically locking them-selves once more. They reached the stone bridge over the stream, Hetty could see that in the middle of the bridge there was a small stone seat.

"Come sit here beside me," said King Frog. "Are you quite comfortable?"

"Oh yes," said Hetty.

"Now, you must keep your eyes closed. I will tell you when to open them."

Hetty nodded, took a deep breath, closing her eyes as tightly as she could.

King Frog reached into his bag and pulled out a handful of sparkling fairy dust. He threw it high up into the air. It gently fell all around them.

"Now, you can open your eyes…"

Chapter 8

Fairyland

Hetty blinked finding herself sitting in a beautiful woodland glade.

"We are here," said King Frog. "Welcome to Fairyland."

Hetty saw something fluttering in the air all around. This time it was not the dragonflies that hovered over Granny's pond, or the little birds in the secret garden where she had made her wish at the wishing well. It was not butterflies, or even the lovely white doves.

It was fairies.

Lots and lots of the sweetest tiny little fairies, wearing such pretty dresses that glowed, twinkled and sparkled in an explosion of colours. It was truly amazing. Hetty felt as if she was sitting right in the middle of a rainbow.

Tiny pixies peeked at her from behind the trees, dressed in bright red jackets with matching red hats, sweet little pixie boots, also trousers in the softest shade of green velvet — just like Hetty had wanted for her old teddybear. She laughed as she watched them dancing and leaping around. They were just so cute and funny.

Amazing bands of coloured light danced and shimmered everywhere.

Hetty gave a sigh. At last, I am here in Fairyland. Gosh, it really is so beautiful. I wish Rosie could be with me now in this magic rainbow land.

"This way," said King Frog, "there is someone waiting to greet you."

Hetty followed, she could not believe her eyes at who was standing before her.

"Goodness, my Mr Christmas!" She gasped.

"Yes, Hetty, your very own Mr Christmas." He smiled. "Welcome to Fairyland. The fairies and pixies are very happy that you are going to join us for this very special tea. There happens to be one very excited little fairy…"

 Suddenly, a rather plump fairy went hurrying past dressed in a cook's outfit, consisting of a large frilly apron and a mop cap made from a white daisy.

"Much to do, so much to do," she muttered. "Hustle and bustle, goodness me, now where are those naughty bees? They are late again with my delivery of honey. The fairy cakes are ready, and the pixies have picked the wild strawberries. We simply must have wild strawberries dipped in honey. Oh my goodness, this is such an important day! Hetty is coming for tea..."

"Hello Hetty, look my wings are dry now. I am now able to fly." A little voice said. "Hold out your hand."

Little Fern fluttered gently down onto her palm.

"Goodness! You are just the most beautiful tiny little fairy."

"Thank you, Hetty, it is so lovely to see you again. Now at last your wish has come true, you are going to have tea with my friends the rainbow pixies and the fairies." She smiled. "But first, I just have to say a big thank you to King Frog. As without him looking after me so well, and making sure I was brought safely home, there might have been a very different ending altogether. Getting wet was very frightening! I have learnt my lesson and will stay away from water in future — forever and ever."

Fern flew over and gave King Frog a big kiss.

"Good heavens, now that is enough of that silly old nonsense." He said, as his face turned from a froggy green to quite a glowing shade of blushing pink. "I must say, my dear Hetty, these little fairies do take a lot of looking after. You see, it is the same thing every year, they can really be quite naughty. Most tiresome indeed."

Hetty giggled as poor King Frog tried to regain his composure, brushing down his jacket, straightening his golden crown, then very quickly standing to attention.

"Now if you don't mind, I feel it's time we got on with things around here." Turning on his heels, he marched on deeper into the woods.

"He is quite a character, don't you think?" Said Mr Christmas. "The fairy folk all love him, even though he is a bit of an old stuffed shirt at times. They trust him, knowing he will always do his best to keep them safe."

"Halt," King Frog called out loudly.

"We are here," said Mr Christmas.

Hetty found herself standing at the top of a beautiful woodland glade gazing down onto a fairy village. All around, there were the sweetest little fairy houses, in the roots of the old trees tiny doors painted in the brightest rainbow colours offered shelter for the pixies.

"Welcome to Fairyland," said Mr Christmas, "the land of make-believe. This way, Hetty. You must meet my rainbow pixies and fairies, the world would be a very dull place without them. You see, they are all my little helpers. We always have so much to get finished before winter, but somehow by Christmas Eve it all seems to fall into place. Everything will be packed, then we will be ready to leave."

Suddenly a loud buzzing sound filled the air.

"Oh look," said fairy Fern, "here come the bees."

"About time," said the cook fairy, still bustling about, "at long last we can all sit down to enjoy our very special tea with Hetty, our most important guest…"

Mr Christmas made a speech to welcome Hetty on behalf of all the pixies and fairies. Everyone gave a big cheer to King Frog for making sure little Fern was brought safely home.

"Oh dear," he muttered, once again looking more than a little flustered.

Hetty thanked everyone for inviting her for tea.

"You see, my Grandma always told me I just had to keep wishing and wishing. Then one day, who knows, my wishes might just come true. Now they have, I am actually here in Fairyland! I know Granny will be so happy to hear my news. Thank you everyone, I will remember this day forever and ever."

Cook fairy arrived with a very large tray of fairy cakes, strawberries and honey.

"There you are now," she smiled as she set everything down. "At last, everyone can enjoy a delicious tea."

"About time too," said King Frog, "I feel am starting to turn quite a pale shade of green. But I am sure some wild strawberries dipped in honey will soon have me back to my old self."

Hetty noticed on the table there was a large pot of strawberry jam.

"You were quite right," said Mr Christmas, "your Aunty does make the most delicious strawberry jam. I must say, I have enjoyed every mouthful."

Hetty laughed. "Poor Aunty Lily, you made her come over all unnecessary when you vanished right before our eyes."

"Yes, I am very sorry about that. You see there is just so much to get finished in time for Christmas. Well as you can tell, dear Hetty, I am not just your Mr Christmas, but Father Christmas to all the children. Very soon it will be time for me to return to Mrs Christmas, Rudolf the Reindeer and all his reindeer friends. As you know, I live in Lapland far, far away from here. It is always very, very cold up there but we are all kept extremely busy reading all your Christmas letters and cards.

"All over the world there are beautiful rainbow fairy villages just like this one. Where the pixies help to gather all the gifts and toys, making sure everything is safely packed ready for me to set off on Christmas Eve. The rainbow fairies find the beautiful red scarlet ribbons to tie up all the gifts."

Hetty noticed a little robin flying past.

"Well," said Father Christmas, "it must be time for him to have his new red breast. He will soon be looking very smart again all ready for winter."

Hetty could not believe her eyes, for there were lots of little robins all standing in a very neat row. The pixies were painting each of their chests with the brightest magic red rainbow paint.

"I love robins," said Hetty, "I often see one in my Daddy's garden."

"That's right, Hetty, you see there are pixies and robins in every garden. Their job is to keep me informed of all the children in the house and, more importantly, whether you are being good children. I must never leave anyone out, so if a new baby arrives the pixies let me know, then I can then add them to my Christmas list. The robin's red breast means they are very important

Christmas helpers." Father Christmas explained. "Hetty, you may have noticed there are lots of red things around in winter. At night, the fairies fly into your gardens to sprinkle fairy dust on the holly trees, turning the holly berries to the brightest red. In fact, there are many trees that have red berries in the cold winter, just to make sure the robins and all the other little birds have plenty of things to eat."

"Gosh that's amazing, we have a holly tree in our garden." Hetty gasped. "And all this happens while I am asleep?"

"Yes that's right," said Father Christmas, "when you are fast asleep, all tucked up in your cosy bed."

"Goodness, I thought only magic things happened on Christmas Eve."

"Now remember, Hetty, whenever you see a rainbow it means the fairies are around — flying through the rainbow from one place to another."

"That's amazing," said Hetty. "I have never thought of that before. Rosie thought rainbows were magic, and now I know they are. She was right after all. The old lady who lives in the watermill, are her lovely ribbons from rainbows too?"

"Yes, dear Hetty, just like your pink ribbon. They are just like the beautiful red ribbons the fairies use to wrap up all the Christmas gifts. Rainbows, pixies and fairies help to make the world a beautiful place." Father Christmas smiled. "Now we must be on our way, I have come here this year to collect my new red tunic. You see it gets very grubby and covered in soot climbing down all the chimneys — though not so many these days, thank goodness. I must say, sometimes my round tummy makes it quite a tight squeeze."

"Father Christmas, how do you manage to climb down a chimney?"

"Well, my dear, once again it is all down to the magic fairy dust. I keep it very safely tucked deep inside my tunic pocket, one sprinkle and I am able to deliver gifts to all the children, even if they don't have a chimney." His eyes twinkled excitedly. "Now, come with me, I think my new tunic must almost be ready."

Hetty's eyes nearly popped out of her head as she spotted the bright red tunic. It seemed to be dancing and floating around in mid-air. The little pixies and fairies were adding the final stitches before sewing on the large round black buttons.

"It's looking wonderful," said Father Christmas, "I am sure it will keep me so very cosy and warm on Christmas Eve. "Thank you all for your hard work, it looks just perfect."

"I must show you the wonderful magic pots. The first one contains magic fairy dust — it helps us fly on Christmas Eve. Look can you see how it sparkles like millions of tiny stars?"

"It's beautiful," said Hetty, "does it help you squeeze down the chimneys too?"

"Yes that's right, now for the pot of magical red paint. Just before we set off on Christmas Eve, when all the toys are safely packed and the reindeer are ready to leave, Rudolf will dip his nose into the magic red paint. Suddenly, his nose will start to glow so brightly it will light up even darkest night sky. So, dear Hetty, do you see how important it is? Without it we would not be able to find our way."

Father Christmas held up the glowing pot of magic red paint.

"As my tunic is almost ready, it will soon be time for me to pop the magic pots deep down into the pockets. Then everything will be ready and it will be time for us all to leave."

The pixies and fairies started to sing…

Rudolf the Red Nosed Reindeer

Has a very shiny nose...

Suddenly something came crashing through the trees. Everyone stopped dancing, laughing and singing. As a huge black rook wearing a golden crown swooped down and seized the little pot of magic red paint. Flying off again screeching and squawking before disappearing into the deep dark woods.

"This really is the most terrible thing," said Father Christmas, "we have to get it back! Without it, we will not able to find our way on Christmas Eve and that will mean there will be no toys for the children on Christmas morning."

The little pixies and fairies started to sob.

"Don't worry," said Hetty, "I am sure we know where he is going, don't we King Frog? Now you must get me back to the watermill as fast as you can."

"Wretched creature," said King Frog, "this is all most infuriating, I must say. Now he has taken things too far, this has to be the most dreadful, unthinkable behaviour. Yes, my dear girl, we must not dilly-dally. Are you ready?"

Hetty nodded.

"Now, close your eyes and count to ten…"

Chapter 9

The rooks' tower

When Hetty opened her eyes she found herself back at the stone bridge.

"Such a miserable state of affairs," mumbled King Frog, "we must try to put a stop to King Rook's most disagreeable and ghastly behaviour, once and for all."

Hetty quickly ran towards the tall gates. They magically flew open to let her through. The old lady was looking very concerned.

"Something really terrible has happened," Hetty sobbed. "King Rook managed to fly right into the fairy village. He swooped down, seized the pot of magic red paint for Rudolf's nose, then disappeared again deep into the dark woods. I really must to try to find it, or Father Christmas will not be able to find his way on Christmas Eve! That means there will be no toys for all the children on Christmas morning."

"Hetty, this is all very upsetting." The old lady gasped.

"Yes it is, but please try not to worry. I am sure I know where he might have taken it. I just need to find my Uncle, I am sure he will know what to do."

As Hetty raced up the lane, she spotted Tom fishing in the stream.

"Tom, please, you must come with me. Something dreadful has happened, we must try to find Uncle Jim."

"Oh thank goodness you are here," gasped Hetty as they arrived at the garage and spotted Uncle Jim.

"My word, young lady, I must say you're looking very upset."

Just then, Rosie came charging into the yard.

"I saw you both running and looking very worried, whatever has happened?"

"Heavens, it is such a long story. I just don't know where to begin!" Hetty gasped.

Uncle Jim gave Hetty a big hug.

"There, little one, just calm down for a moment. Now take your time, start from the very beginning. Then we can make up our minds as to what we can do."

"I just hope you believe me, it all sounds more than a little bit crazy." Hetty began. "Well first, I tied my magic pink ribbon into my hair, then I quickly made my way down to the old watermill. It was there I met King Frog. He always wears his beautiful golden crown and speaks in such a very posh way."

Tom and Rosie exchanged confused glances.

"It's true," said Hetty, "honest, cross my heart."

"Go on, lass, just carry on." Said Uncle Jim.

"Well, Tom, do you remember the first time we went down to the mill? We met the old lady, we both felt very disappointed that she was not a witch after all."

"That's right," said Tom. "Afterwards, we strolled back up the lane eating our apples. Hetty, if I remember, you felt very tired and just wanted to sit down to paddle your feet in the stream. Then I went off to find my friends to see if they wanted to play a game of cricket."

"Well that's it," said Hetty. "After you left, that is when all the real magic started to happen. As I was sitting there, I thought I could hear someone crying. Suddenly I could not believe my eyes, for there sitting on a lily pad was a beautiful tiny little fairy. The little fairy is called Fern, Rosie, she is just so sweet and adorable. She was very upset because her wings had become so wet she was not able to fly home. That's when King Frog came to her rescue. King Frog blew his whistle then, to my utter amazement, a large grey rabbit leapt out from the hedgerow. Little fairy Fern clambered onto the rabbit's back. Then King Frog asked the rabbit if he would be so kind as to take the little fairy safely home, hopefully in time for her to enjoy a most delightful tea! Afterwards, King Frog chatted to me for a little while. He thought it was all an extremely good job well done, but before I could say anything else he just hopped off and disappeared back into the hedgerow. That's when Beth found me, but when I told her the story she thought I had had too much sun. I thought perhaps I might have fallen asleep, and that it was all just a lovely dream after all. I had to find out more. So today, making sure I was wearing my pink ribbon, I went back. Sitting myself down by the stream, I whispered 'King Frog, are you there?' Then he leapt out from the hedgerow and we chatted for a while about all sorts of things. He announced he had an invitation for me to have tea with the fairies."

"Goodness, how amazing," Rosie giggled.

"First we went to the watermill, where the old lady greeted us. She was very happy for me, because my wishes were about to come true."

"What happened next?" asked Rosie.

"Well, Tom, do you remember the tall gates on the edge of the castle woods? Somehow they just magically unlocked themselves to allow us through into the castle grounds. As soon as we entered, I watched as the gates slowly closed, firmly locking once more."

"That's real magic," gasped Rosie. "Were you scared?"

"Just a little," said Hetty.

"Go on, lass," said Uncle Jim, "we need to get to the bottom of this."

"We made our way over to the stone bridge. I had to sit on the little stone seat next to him then close my eyes as tightly as I could. When I opened my eyes, I found we were in the most beautiful woodland glade, it was truly amazing —glowing in all the colours of the rainbow. Rosie, it really is the most wonderful magic rainbow land."

"Hetty, that all sounds completely bonkers," said Tom.

"It sure does, but you must agree very, very magic too." Sighed Rosie.

"First I met Mr Christmas and little fairy Fern. We walked to the fairy village where we all enjoyed a most delicious tea. There were pixies, fairies and lots of other little woodland creatures. After tea, Mr Christmas told me he was not just my Mr Christmas, he is Father Christmas to all the children all over the world."

"Awesome," said Tom, "is this true? Cross your heart and hope to die?"

"Honestly, yes it is true," said Hetty.

"I think I am going to faint," said Rosie.

"Now carry on, lass," said Uncle Jim, "we just need to find out why you are so upset. So just calm down and take your time."

"Well, Father Christmas told me all about the rainbow pixies and fairies. You see, they are all his little Christmas helpers. Of course I must not forget the robins, but I think I will have to tell you about them some other time. Father Christmas wanted to take me to see the finishing touches being added to his beautiful new red tunic. It was truly amazing, floating around in mid-air. Little pixies were busy sewing on the large round black buttons, and the little fairies just need to add the warm fur around the hood to make it perfect, ready for Father Christmas to take home all the way to Lapland. You see, there is just so much to get finished in time for Christmas Eve.

"Fairy Fern wanted to show me the two most important things

that would be placed in each of the pockets. Father Christmas held up two little pots for me to see. He explained the first one contained magic fairy dust, he just has to sprinkle it all over him so then he is able to deliver toys to all the children on Christmas Eve — even if they don't have a chimney. It was sparkling like thousands and thousands of silver stars.

"That sounds awesome," said Tom. "Hetty, you must tell us what was in the other little pot."

"It was magic red paint. Father Christmas held it up for us all to see, at that moment the most truly dreadful thing happened. King Rook came crashing through the trees, he seized the little pot from Father Christmas then flew off again into the deep dark woods. Everyone started to cry, honestly it was such a fright. Truly horrid."

"But Hetty, you must tell us why it is so important to find it."

"Because, Tom, it's the magic red paint for Rudolph's nose. It lights up the sky on Christmas Eve, so without it Father Christmas will not be able to find his way. That will mean there will be no toys for all the children on Christmas morning."

"Oh heavens!" Tom said Rosie. "You know the song — 'Rudolph the red nosed reindeer, has a very shiny nose…"

"That's a tough one," said Uncle Jim. "So where do you think he has taken it?"

"To the tower, Uncle Jim, he must have taken it to the tower. King Rook lives up there with all his horrid friends. Oh Tom, do you remember how scared we were at the tower?"

"Goodness yes, I remember." Shivered Rosie. "Full of huge squawking black rooks with their horrid shiny black feathers…"

"Now I am going to have to give this some serious thought," said Uncle Jim.

The children watched as he paced up and down the yard, stopping now and again to mop his brow with a large red and white spotted hankie.

Hetty started to cry, while Rosie and Tom stared anxiously at each other.

"Don't worry, Het," Tom said, "I am sure your Uncle will come up with a good plan. Fingers crossed."

Uncle Jim took a few more thoughtful moments before speaking.

"Well, young Hetty, you see in my mind the best way forward is to catch those blighters off guard. Now, as I am such a very clever old Uncle Jim, in the back of my old garage we might just find the very thing to sort this problem out. You see, my old starting pistol — that ought to do the trick to scare them right enough. I sometimes use it to keep the rooks off my garden, but this time we need to teach them all a lesson, once and for all. Cheer up, young Hetty, we have a job to do — no time to dilly-dally. You must all listen to me very carefully now, we need to work together as a team, do you understand?"

"Oh goodness, yes, we will do anything. We promise." Said Hetty, quickly wiping away her tears in the hem of her skirt.

"Now if you are ready, we can be on our way. I must say it has been a long time since I climbed up to the tower, my poor old knees sure give me some jip these days, but let's hope we can get the job done. Tom, you go and find the towing rope in the garage — we might need it. Those pesky rooks have been causing no end of trouble in the village for as far back as I can remember."

"I am sure King Rook and his horrid friends will be up in the tower right now, shrieking and squawking." Said Rosie.

"Well there is only one way to find out, come on young shipmates, let's be on our way."

Soon they arrived at the winding path leading up to the tower.

"Just wait here for a moment," said Uncle Jim. "Now, make sure you keep right behind me, and as quiet as three church mice. Do you understand?"

The children all nodded in agreement. Creeping very slowly, they started to make their climb up the steep overgrown path. Hetty and Rosie glanced at each other, remembering how frightened they had been the last time they were here in the creepy tower woods, surrounded by hundreds of swaying creaking trees, squeezing past the thick bushes and scratchy ferns.

"Ouch!" Yelped Rosie, as she stepped into a bed of nettles.

"Shush children! We are almost at the tower. Now I want you all to get down as low as you can, we need to creep very slowly and quietly forward…"

"We've made it," whispered Tom as a clearing came into view.

The huge tower stood before them. They watched as hundreds of black rooks swooped and squawked with gleeful excitement high overhead. Suddenly they all flew back, quickly settling into the nooks and crannies of the tower. Immediately, the noise and squawking stopped.

The children were too scared to move a muscle. They could feel their hearts thumping deep in their chest as the wood instantly fell silent.

"Look," whispered Hetty. "I can see King Rook halfway up the tower, his golden crown is glinting in the sunshine."

Suddenly he took off, making loud shrills of gleeful triumph. He swirled high over the tower, then with a whoosh he swooped down and seized something in his long sharp claws.

"I am sure that must be the little pot of magic paint," whispered Tom. "Look, I can see it glowing from here."

"Time for action," said Uncle Jim. "Let's hope this is going to work. Children, put your hands over your ears — this is going to be very loud."

Taking the pistol from his pocket, he pointed it at the tower.

BANG, BANG! went the gun.

The sound echoed through the woods.

"One more for luck."

BANG! went the pistol again.

"Now children, leap out and make as much noise as you can. Jump up and down and wave your arms in the air."

The rooks took off in all directions, squawking and screeching with fright.

"Did you see that?" Called out Hetty. "King Rook dropped something from his claws... Yes! Look! There it is, I can see it twinkling high up on a ledge."

"Right children, come on. Let's just see if we can pull this off. Tom, hand me the rope. Now, I am going to try and throw it up as high as I can. Hopefully, with any luck, it will lodge into a gap between the stones."

It seemed to take ages.

"Well now, that seems to have done the trick." Said Uncle Jim. "What a bit of luck, it's just in the right place. Hang on a minute, young Tom, I need to give it a tug to make sure it is firm enough to take your weight."

"Goodness Tom, I do hope you can climb up that high." Said Hetty.

"Don't worry, lass, at his age he will be as fit as a flea — just like I used to be. Do you think you can pull yourself up?"

"Yes," said Tom, "I am quite strong."

Slowly and carefully, Tom started to heave himself up. His feet slipped on the green moss as he climbed, sending small pieces of loose stone bouncing down the tower wall.

"Steady my lad," called Uncle Jim. "Now girls, make sure you keep back out of the way, I don't want you getting hurt."

Tom suddenly came to a halt.

"I can't climb any higher, I am at the end of the rope." His call echoed through the woods.

"Oh goodness, what are we going to do now?" Gasped Hetty.

"Tom, it's alright. You are just below the ledge," said Uncle Jim. "Hold on as tightly as you can, now just see if you can reach up over the ledge. You're only a couple of inches away."

Tom wriggled himself up a little higher.

"It's no use! I can just about touch it with my fingertips, but not enough to pick it up."

"Oh goodness, we just have to take it back." Said Hetty bursting into tears. "I wish… I wish… I wish… there was someone who could help."

"Please don't cry," said Rosie, giving Hetty a big hug. "Here, use my hankie. I am sure everything will be fine, we just have to find another way."

For a moment, a hush fell over the wood. Not a sound could be heard.

"Listen," said Rosie, suddenly leaping to her feet. "Hetty, I can hear something."

"Look everyone!" Called Tom. "Doves! I can see lots of white doves."

Hetty started to laugh through her tears as the doves fluttered all around like a beautiful white cloud, before gently settling into trees.

"You made your second wish, Hetty," the doves cooed, "so we are here to make your wish to come true."

Rosie could not believe her eyes or her ears. "This is amazing! Talking doves! This is so magical, is this really happening?"

"It sure is," said Uncle Jim. "Now doves, if you would be so kind? I think our young Tom could do with a bit of a hand up there."

"Oh yes please, lovely doves, please can you help?" Giggled Hetty.

This is truly bonkers, thought Tom, trying to grasp the fact he had just heard the doves talk to Hetty while trying not to fall.

One of the doves flew up to the ledge where a very confused Tom was waiting.

"Afternoon to you, Mrs Dove," said Tom. He wasn't sure what to say, seeing as he had never had a conversation with a dove before. "You see Mrs Dove, I can almost reach the little magic pot but not enough to pick it up, do you think you could nudge it forward with your beak? That's brilliant, just a little bit more. Hetty look! I've got it! Goodness, it is incredible. Look how brightly it glows!"

"Steady, my lad." Uncle Jim called. "Now, make sure you push it down deep into your pocket and hold on as tightly as you can."

Tom carefully lowered himself gently to the ground.

"Come on," said Rosie, "let's have a look."

Tom pulled the little pot from his pocket, holding it up for all to see.

"Wow!"

"Amazing!"

"Just look how it glows!"

"Tom, you were brilliant." Said Hetty, giving him a big hug. "Now, we must take it back right away, everyone will be very worried."

"Don't worry Hetty, a message will be sent to the fairy village. This is such a wonderful day, everyone will be so happy and excited. Some other little woodland friends have also come to say thank you."

The children could not believe their eyes, as out from the hedgerow hopped some little rabbits, a hedgehog, a badger, then a fox, even a very shy deer crept gently forward. The trees were suddenly full of chattering little birds, last of all the wise old owl swooped down.

"Thank you, dear children, this has been a great achievement. Without your help, Christmas would never have been the same again. You see, I live way up in the castle turrets. From there, I can keep watch over everything. So now it will be my great honour to once more bring law and order at last back to the village."

The old owl ruffled his feathers puffing out his chest importantly.

"I proclaim, most profoundly, from this day forward: King Rook, or any other rook for that matter, must never ever enter the castle woods or the fairy village again. The tower woods will be their home and there they must stay forever."

"Thank you so much, wise Owl," said Hetty, "the fairies will be so happy."

"Now it is time to take you back, everyone will be waiting to greet you. So children, gather around, make sure your eyes are tightly closed."

"Wow, amazing!" Said Tom. "Look! We are all back at the old watermill, how did that happen?"

"Yes, and very welcome you are too," said King Frog. "You have all managed to achieve an absolutely splendid and magnificent job, hats off to you all."

Rosie and Tom were speechless...

Chapter 10
The Fairy Queen

"Let me introduce you to King Frog," said Hetty. "King Frog looks after the fairies and the castle woods — that's an extremely and most important job, don't you think?"

"Yes indeed. A most important job," agreed King Frog.

"Very pleased to meet you," said Rosie and Tom.

"And this is my Uncle Jim."

"Hello," said Uncle Jim, "it's good to see you again, King Frog."

"Again?" Gasped Hetty. "You've met before?"

"Yes that's right," said Uncle Jim, "a very long time ago now. I was just a young lad at the time — about your age, Hetty."

"Goodness! So that is how you knew all about my magic pink ribbon."

"That's right, don't you remember I told you your Grandma was given a pink ribbon just like yours?"

"Goodness Uncle Jim, now I know why Granny believes in fairies! She met them with you when she was a little girl."

"Yes that's right, Hetty, we also met the old lady who lives in the mill and all your rainbow pixies and fairies."

Tom turned to the old lady, who was waiting for them by the gates.

"But you're not really a witch after all, are you?" said Tom.

The old lady smiled.

"How do you know that?" Asked Rosie.

"Well Rosie, you see Hetty and I came down to the watermill just a few days ago."

"It was very scary at first, as we thought we might be turned into toads. Instead, we were invited in, and the old lady shared a few very top secrets that we must never tell to anyone."

"Goodness," said Rosie, "this has been a very magic day. I wonder what will happen next?"

"Well I think it has been a most infuriating carry on, if you ask me." Said King Frog. "This sort of thing is most unsettling, but all in all it has been a most wonderful and agreeable outcome indeed. Hurry this way children, no time to shilly-shally. You have all been invited to have tea with the fairies, now time is getting on — we don't want to be late. I must say, I do rather enjoy a lovely cream tea, don't you? Most importantly, we must return the wonderful pot of magic paint. Come this way, children, keep up."

Hetty glanced towards Uncle Jim.

"Go on, off you go, lass, I will wait here with the old lady and hope I don't get turned into a toad."

"Oh yes," said the old lady, "it will be very nice to have some company for a change. We can both enjoy a lovely cup of my green witch's tea."

With this, King Frog turned on his heels and marched towards the tall gates, magically they flew open to let them through.

Tom had to grab hold of Rosie to slow her down, she was so full of magic she looked as though she might burst with excitement.

"Best foot forward, children, follow me." King Frog said as the gates closed behind them, firmly locking once again.

Hetty ran towards the bridge.

"Come on, you two, we have to sit on this little seat."

"This is awesome," said Tom.

"That's right, children, now bunch up, close your eyes as tightly as you can. Are you ready?"

"Yes," Hetty whispered.

King Frog reached deep down into his bag and took out a large handful of fairy dust. He threw it high into the air.

Twiddle-le dumb... twiddle–le dee...
Take us to fairyland for tea.

"Welcome, children, you can now open your eyes."

Standing before them was Father Christmas.

Tom and Rosie were speechless.

"Welcome to you both," he said, holding out his hands to greet them. "I would like to say thank you. For this is a very special day, one that will go down in fairy history. But our most sincere thanks must go to our dear Hetty. You, my dear, have accomplished something quite wonderful. Now Christmas can be perfect once more."

"I am just so happy it all worked out so well," said Hetty. "I think Tom has something for you."

Tom handed the twinkling pot of magic red paint to Father Christmas.

"Thank you, Tom. Now, we must make sure this is kept very safe." Father Christmas smiled.

Rosie couldn't help jumping up and down. She was so happy.

"I must tell you, Father Christmas, we met the wise old owl." Rosie said. "Gosh! It is so wonderful, you see he has made a new law to banish King Rook and all the other rooks from the castle and castle woods forever and ever."

"Well, my dear children, this is most welcome news. Now, at last, everyone can live in peace and be happy ever after."

King Frog cleared his throat and gave very polite cough, puffing out his chest to such an extent he looked as if he might just go pop.

"This has been a most extraordinary day, don't you think? But now ending in the most splendid way….

> So off to the Fairy village we must go
>
> Put your best foot forward, don't be slow
>
> March behind me one, two, three
>
> Are you ready? Keep up with me

Off they all marched one, two, three.

"Halt!" said King Frog. "Now, children, once more you must close your eyes."

From his little bag came more sparkling fairy dust. And then…

"Welcome to Fairyland," said Father Christmas, "the land of make believe."

"Goodness, it's a rainbow land," gasped Rosie, "a real magic rainbow land."

For a moment, Tom just stood open-mouthed, then he whispered;

"Wow, this is truly awesome!"

Suddenly, the air was full of little fairies.

"Hello," said Rosie, "you must be the rainbow fairies. How pretty you look in your dresses in all the colours of the rainbow. You really are the sweetest little things I have ever seen. I would love to meet fairy Fern."

"I am just here, Rosie, hold out your hand."

Fairy Fern gently landed on her palm.

"Hello," Rosie smiled. "Hetty has told me all about you. I am so happy your wings are dry."

"Yes, and it is all thanks to King Frog." Fern replied. "He is quite wonderful, don't you think? We all love him very dearly, even though sometimes he can become quite cross. You see, without King Frog to keep a watchful eye on things around here, I think our lives would just be all so topsy-turvy."

"Balderdash." Said King Frog. "Now that is enough of that sloppy old nonsense. Let's be on our way. We have a magnificent tea waiting for us."

"How absolutely wonderful, don't you think?" Said Fern with a little teasing giggle.

"Infuriating fairies," he huffed and puffed, "such a lively bunch this year, I must say. I find it all extremely tiresome, quite exhausting indeed."

The little pixies, (all dressed in their red tunics and pixie boots), danced merrily around. Tom sat one on each of his shoulders as they made their way towards the fairy village.

Everyone enjoyed the most amazing party, with lots of delicious things to eat — but most importantly, the fairy cakes with sweet wild strawberries dipped in honey.

Then it was time for Father Christmas to try on his new red tunic.

It fitted him perfectly.

"You look wonderful," said Hetty. "At last, you are all ready for Christmas."

"Hetty, don't you think you have forgotten the two most important things?" Asked one of the little pixies.

"Oh gosh!" Said Hetty. "The magic pots! How could we have forgotten them? After all, they are the reason we are here."

King Frog handed the pots to Hetty. "I think, my dear, you should have this honour."

Hetty gently placed a magic pot one into in each pocket of Father Christmas's tunic.

"There now, at last you are utterly and truly ready for Christmas." She declared.

"Hooray!"

Everyone laughed and cheered, then started to sing...

Rudolf the red nosed reindeer

Has a very shiny nose...

Suddenly King Frog leapt onto a toadstool, blowing his whistle loudly.

"Attention! Attention everyone," he called. "All please be upstanding."

The children were spellbound. As through a mystical fountain of white light, brighter than the brightest twinkling stars, the Fairy Queen appeared before them. She wore a dazzling diamond crown and her beautiful silver gown was sparkling with clusters of shimmering crystals. A magnificent long cape floated gently behind her, glowing in the deepest shade of purple velvet.

The children were speechless, staring in utter amazement.

"It's the Fairy Queen," whispered Fern.

The Fairy Queen waved her magic wand, sending what looked like shimmering silver raindrops tumbling to the ground. The children gasped, totally bewitched, as the Fairy Queen glided gracefully towards them.

> Hello, dear children, I have come to say,
> Thank you for this perfect day
> A happy ending for one and all,
> Tonight we will hold a fairy ball
> You must all keep the secret of this fairyland,
> Hidden deep in the castle grounds.
> Take care, dear children, now I must go
> One day we all might meet again
> Who knows...

She waved her magic wand, and in a flash of light she was gone.

"Oh my goodness," said Hetty, "she is so beautiful."

"Oh yes," said Father Christmas, "you have all been truly honoured. You see, children…

> Very few ever meet the Fairy Queen,
>
> Just think how lucky you have been.
>
> For now it is time for us to leave
>
> Remember to look out for me on Christmas Eve.
>
> Rudolf will be pleased to know
>
> We will now find our way again through the snow.
>
> Take care dear Hetty, Rosie, and Tom
>
> When you wake in the morning, we will all be gone.

"Just remember, the rainbow fairies are never far away."

"Goodbye Hetty," said fairy Fern, "make sure you wear your magic ribbon just one more time — on Christmas day. Who knows, you might find a little gift from me…"

"Come children," said King Frog, "it is time for us to leave. Now please close your eyes and count to ten."

"Wow look," said Tom, "we are back again."

"That was the best magic day ever," said Rosie.

"Yes it was," giggled Hetty.

The children watched in wonder as the tall gates once again slowly opened for them.

"Welcome back," said Uncle Jim, "you look as if you have all enjoyed a wonderful day."

"Oh yes," said Hetty. "We had the most lovely party with Father Christmas, the pixies, fairies and lots of other little woodland creatures. Then the most exciting thing happened, the Fairy Queen came to greet us."

"Goodness! You have all been truly blessed," said the old lady.

"Yes, one mustn't complain," announced King Frog. "After all, a visitation from the Fairy Queen made it a most enchanting, delightful, a truly splendid day indeed. Bravo everyone, for getting an exceedingly good job done. Now Christmas will be perfect once more, all full of laughter and fun. What a brave bunch you have been. At last, the ghastly rooks are banished from Fairyland forever."

"Thank you, King Frog," said Hetty. "I always wished that one day I would meet some little fairies, well now I have. And it's all thanks to you."

"It has been a pleasure, dear Hetty, now I must not dilly-dally. It is time for me to take my leave, I have my duties that must be done. It has been quite wonderful to share such fun. Take care, dear children. Good to meet you too, Rosie and Tom. Goodbye everyone." Then in a flash he was gone.

"What a wonderful day," sighed Hetty. "This has been the best holiday ever. Goodbye old lady, I will treasure my magic pink ribbon and I will keep the secret of the castle woods locked in my heart forever."

"My dear Hetty, I am so happy. For now all your wishes have

come true." The old lady smiled. "Thank you too, Rosie and Tom, for all your help. At last, a happy ending."

"It really has been the best magic day ever," said Rosie.

"For me too," said Tom, "now even I can say I believe in Fairies."

"Well, what a day this has turned out to be." Said Uncle Jim as they made their way back up the lane. "You must never tell a soul, it must remain our secret. Do you understand?"

"Yes, we promise, cross our hearts."

As they entered the village, it seemed even more beautiful on this lovely summer's day. With its cobbled pavements, and the pretty cottages with their window boxes full of summer flowers glowing brightly in the warm sunshine. People were enjoying ice creams or creamy fudge. Ladies were busily getting the old Yarn Market ready for market day.

Hetty sighed as she gazed up at the castle, knowing somewhere high in the turrets the wise old owl would be gazing down.

"Look at the tower," said Tom, "I can see the rooks swirling around the tree tops."

"Yes, and they can stay up there too." Said Uncle Jim. "No more pecking at my strawberries! Now, if nothing else, that will be a happy ending..."

Chapter 11

Home

Sadly, Hetty's holiday was almost over.

Poor Aunty Lily could not help wondering why Hetty was spending so much time brushing her hair until it was shining and tangle free. All very peculiar, she thought, the two of them exchanged glances as if they were sharing a secret.

In fact, there had been many strange things happening over the last two weeks. Imaginary nonsense, I am sure of it, she thought. Even so, she had to admit it did all seem very mysterious and quite unnerving at times. People don't just disappear, do they? Well bless my soul, it seems they do! Young Hetty's Mr Christmas certainly did. That is a lot for me to take in, so it must be time for me to enjoy a nice lovely cup of tea.

Hetty, Tom and Rosie, along with Beth and Ruth, met up at the beach for the last time. They wandered along the shoreline, picking up shells washed in by the tide.

"I will take these home with me," said Hetty, "they will remind me of this amazing holiday."

"It has been very special, and very magic too." Said Tom.

"It sure has." Said Rosie, giving Hetty a knowing wink. "Don't you think it would be great if we could all meet up again next summer?"

"That would be wonderful," said the twins, "let's all shake on it."

The time came for Hetty to pack her things back into her red case. Her old teddy bear and her magic pink ribbon were the last to be carefully tucked inside.

"Thank you, pink ribbon, thank you for everything." She whispered.

Later that evening, Hetty was sitting at the kitchen table having supper with Aunty Lily and Uncle Jim. Smudge was sleeping soundly in his basket. She felt a little sad that her holiday was over, even though it would be lovely to see Mummy and Daddy again. It had been the best holiday ever. At last, Hetty had at met her fairy friends, King Frog, and not forgetting her very own Mr Christmas.

"Thank you both for my lovely holiday," said Hetty, "I would love to stay with you again next year."

"I see no reason why not," said Uncle Jim.

"Well, dear Jim, I think we are going to miss our little maid next week. Although I must say, it has all been a bit of a rumpus. When I think about that Mr Christmas at the market, with him being there one minute and gone the next, it makes me come over all funny peculiar."

Hetty and Uncle Jim fell about laughing.

Old Smudge woke up and began to bark, chasing around the kitchen.

"Here we go again, more rumpus!" Said Aunty Lily.

They all laughed until their sides ached.

The next morning, Hetty's Mummy arrived. It was so lovely to see her again.

"Goodness Hetty, you look as if you have had a wonderful time." Mummy said.

"She sure has." Said Uncle Jim, giving Hetty a knowing wink.

"Secrets," said Aunty Lily, "that's all we have had. Secrets. Goodness knows what has been going on, they are as bad as each other."

When it was time for Hetty to leave, Uncle Jim arrived with his huge shiny black taxi.

"Nothing but the best for my very important customer."

"Honestly May, it has been like this for the last two weeks," said Aunty Lily.

Uncle Jim gave a salute while holding the car door open for Mummy and Hetty to slide onto the very large comfortable rear seat.

"I feel just like a princess," said Hetty.

"Well then, your highness, I will drive you to meet your train right away."

"Jim Parsons, you do get more like a big child every day. Honest to goodness, May, the two of them never stop larking about."

"Come on, Lily, climb aboard." Uncle Jim grinned. "You too,

Smudge, you had best come and see our Hetty off."

With the huge red case placed safely in the boot, it was time to leave. Smudge loved to poke his head out of the window and bark loudly. His long ears flapped in the wind as they drove to the station.

"As you can see, dear May, he really loves a nice ride in the car." Uncle Jim laughed.

"He is such a funny old dog," said Hetty. "I will miss taking him to the beach with Rosie and Tom."

"Never mind," said Uncle Jim, "there will always be next time."

"I wonder if we will see your Mr Christmas on the train today?" Enquired Mummy.

"No, not today," said Hetty. "You see, he has already travelled all the way home to Lapland. He has a lot to do before Christmas, it all keeps him very busy."

"Goodness me, how would you know such things?"

"Oh, it's just that a little fairy told me," she giggled.

"Yes, that is quite true," agreed Uncle Jim.

"May, you see? Off again with secrets, nothing but secrets." Aunty Lily sighed.

The station was very busy. Everyone looked as if they had enjoyed a lovely holiday. Hetty was feeling sad that her holiday was over, but she soon forgot about all that when she saw the train in the distance, puffing along the track from Minehead. Steam from its chimney was leaving huge fluffy white clouds in the sky.

"Goodness I am really looking forward to seeing Daddy, but thank you so much for letting me stay it has been the best holiday ever."

"Well you can come to stay whenever you wish, dear Hetty," said Uncle Jim. "Now enjoy a safe journey home, and give our love to your Daddy."

"I think he has really missed you," said Mummy.

"So will we," said Aunty Lily, "the old cottage will seem very quiet again without you."

As the steam train rumbled into the station, Hetty gave a big sigh. She thought about what a magical time she had had since the last time she was on the train. Her wishes had come true — it had been a truly wonderful holiday.

"I think Dunster is the most special magical place, don't you Mummy?"

"Well, I know your Grandma certainly thinks so, ever since she was a little girl."

"Oh yes. Now we know why, don't we Uncle Jim?" Hetty grinned, giving him a wink.

The Station Master blew his whistle with a piercing shrill.

"Climb aboard, everyone, move along now." He called. "There will be plenty of room, we have put extra carriages on today."

Hetty hugged Aunty Lily and Uncle Jim. Then she gave Smudge a big kiss and he licked her face.

"You are such a funny old dog, I am going to miss you but

I promise we will take you to the beach next time."

Hetty jumped on board the train sitting herself by the window.

"Well May, next time you must all come down," Aunty Lily said to Mummy, "then we can enjoy a lovely drive or a picnic right at the top of Exmoor."

"We would love that, Aunty Lily, perhaps after Christmas. Or maybe in the spring when moor will be covered in flowers and the new Exmoor ponies will be born. That really would be lovely."

As the train puffed out of the station, Hetty waved blowing kisses until Aunty Lily, Uncle Jim, and Smudge were out of sight.

"We have really missed you," said Mummy.

"I have missed you too." Said Hetty, giving Mummy a big hug. "I can't wait to give Daddy a big hug too. I am looking forward to see my old friends, I have so much to tell them."

All the way home, Hetty chatted about her holiday. She told Mummy all about her new friends, especially Rosie and Tom.

Daddy was waiting to greet them at the station. Hetty ran along the platform and leapt into his arms.

"Goodness, you look happy. You must have enjoyed a wonderful time, I am looking forward to hearing all about it." Daddy said as he gave her a huge hug.

A porter came along with a trolley to help with Hetty's huge red case.

"Well, dear Hetty, do tell me — did you need all those things after all?"

"No, not really Daddy, you see the sun shone every day so I was able to go out and play with my new friends. We had such a magical time, I can't wait to tell Granny all my exciting news."

It was so good to be home again. Later that evening, Hetty snuggled down in her comfy bed with her old teddy tucked firmly under her arm. She made sure her magic pink ribbon was gently placed under her pillow.

She soon fell fast asleep and dreamed about the little pixies, fairies, King Frog, the old lady who lived in the mill, fairy Fern, and Mr Christmas…

> Dreaming such magical dreams
> Meeting the Fairy Queen
> Oh how lucky she had been
> Sweet wild strawberries dipped in honey
> Little robins too
> The wishing well, castle, and tower
> The horrid black rooks, now banished forever,
> So many wonderful things to remember for ever and ever.
> Not forgetting the beautiful white doves,
> and still one last wish to come.
> Goodness I wonder what it will be,
> I will just have to wait and see!

Chapter 12

Christmas

The following morning, Jill and Sue (Hetty's best friends), came over to play. They couldn't wait to hear all about Hetty's holiday.

"Oh goodness, it was just the best holiday ever! Dunster truly is the most magical place. I made a wish at the wishing well — now I know when you make a wish, your wishes can actually come true. I also met lots of new friends. When I go back next summer I will be able to see Rosie and Tom again, we shared the most amazing secret adventure. afterwards we all had to cross our hearts and promise we would never ever tell anyone. It must remain our secret forever and ever. But it is so good to be home again. After all, you are my very best friends."

"Please Hetty," asked Jill, "can we go down to your playhouse? I would love to play dressing up."

"Yes, let's do that," said Hetty.

The girls ran down the garden, quickly gathering around the old wooden dressing up chest. Hetty opened the lid, gently lifting out her most treasured possession, her Great Grandma's deep purple velvet cape.

"Goodness," said Sue, "look! There is something else. I can see it glowing deep down inside the box."

They all gasped.

Underneath all the other things, sparkling like the brightest star, was the most beautiful silver dress covered in silver sequins and shining crystals.

Hetty held it up, "Oh my goodness! How did that get in here?"

"Wow!" Said her friends, "it looks just like a Fairy Queen's dress."

"Look there is something else in here too."

Jill lifted out a silver crown, then a beautiful long flowing cape made from the deepest shade of purple velvet. It was edged in silver crystals.

Gone was the old wooden spoon, in its place was a sparkling silver wand.

"Wow! Where did it all come from?" Gasped the girls.

Hetty giggled, "I think it must be a gift from some of my little magic friends, that is all I am able to say."

"Oh Hetty, they are the most beautiful things we have ever seen. You must try it on."

Everything fitted her like a dream. When Hetty stepped out into the sunlight, even the boys who lived next door were (for once) lost for words.

Hetty danced around the garden waving her magic silver wand and singing.

> What a magical day this has been
> I look just like the Fairy Queen!

The next Sunday morning, Hetty was very excited. Granny had invited everyone for afternoon tea, at last, Hetty would be able to tell her all about her amazing magical holiday.

It was so lovely to be at Granny's again.

"Come in, everyone, it is so good to see you. It feels like a very special day," she said, "so I thought for a change it would be lovely to have tea in the sitting room."

Granny's lovely round mahogany table looked wonderful covered in the most delicate white tablecloth edged in wide lace. As always, it was full of the most delicious things to eat. The French doors were wide open, allowing the sweet smell of roses and honeysuckle to gently drift into the room.

"Hetty, you may have noticed that I have not made you a chocolate cake this time," said Granny. "You see, I thought for a change you might enjoy a sponge cake topped with cream, with wild strawberries dipped in honey. It is something I enjoyed once, many years ago with some very special little friends. I think your Uncle Jim might have enjoyed it too when he was a little boy."

"Oh yes, Granny, he told me all about it."

"Now, young lady, perhaps after tea you would like to join me for a walk around the garden? We could sit by the lily pond, then you can tell me all about your holiday."

"The flowers look so bright today, don't you think? Granny, did you know that is all down to the little fairies?"

"Yes, little one, and many more wonderful things too." Granny smiled. "Come and sit with me, let us both enjoy this lovely summers day."

"This is where it all began," said Hetty, "I was sitting here watching the dragonflies hovering over the water lilies thinking they looked just like little fairies. Oh Granny, it has been so wonderful. First I met my Mr Christmas, then King Frog and little fairy Fern…" Hetty continued to tell her Grandma all the magical things that had happened.

"Dear Hetty," Granny said when she had finished. "I just knew if you truly believed, one day your wishes would come true. What a lucky girl you have been. It all must remain our secret forever, we have both been truly blessed. Just to think, it was all down to our magic pink ribbons."

"Granny, I was wondering, where did you find the wild strawberries and honey?"

"Well, would you believe it, my dear child? They were sitting on my doorstep this very morning. I think they could be a delicious gift from some of our little fairy friends, don't you?"

The summer holiday was soon over, and it was time for Hetty and her friends to return to school.

Once more, she enjoyed her dancing class on Saturday mornings, but life would never be quite the same again. For now she noticed how bright the flowers were, and always made sure there was always plenty of food left out for the birds. Sometimes she would see a robin in Daddy's garden, looking very smart with his lovely new shiny red breast. Hetty would always give him a little wave and whisper "hello".

"It feels a lot colder today," said Mummy, "I think it is time to get out the winter coats, hats and gloves, then we can warm them by the fire."

They both gazed out of the window, and noticed the holly tree was now completely covered in bright red berries.

"How lovely it looks," said Mummy, "now autumn is truly here."

Hetty remembered the fairies must have sprinkled it with fairy dust during the night when everyone was fast asleep.

The leaves on the trees were also starting to change colour, from green to bright crimson or gold. Before long, the cold east wind would arrive sending the leaves gently fluttering to the ground, leaving a crimson carpet across the land. Hetty loved walking through the rustling leaves.

Mr Christmas had told her all about the trees. It would soon be time for them to slowly fall asleep, a long sleep all through the cold winter. The thought of snow and ice made Hetty shiver. Christmas will soon be here, she thought, I do hope Father Christmas will be all cosy and warm in his smart new red tunic, and that they will be able to find their way with Rudolf's bright new shiny nose.

Looking back, her holiday seemed just like a dream — a wonderful magic dream. But she still had her pink ribbon, and she would wear it just once more on Christmas Day.

Hetty was feeling very happy, there were lots of things going on at her school. The choir were rehearsing Christmas carols, everyone was trying to remember their lines for the Christmas play, there were lots of new costumes to be made. The huge Christmas tree arrived, standing proudly in the school hall. The little first year children were allowed to arrange the twinkling decorations, but the tree was so tall that the poor Headmaster had to climb to the top of the caretaker's ladder to place the shining star right on to the top.

Hetty thought it looked wonderful. But, of course, Hetty would have preferred to have a fairy on the top of the tree.

Later that evening Daddy arrived home with a beautiful Christmas tree.

They all enjoyed eating mince pies, the tree was decorated, and yes complete with a little Fairy on the top!

The school Christmas play and carol singing were all a great success. At last, the Christmas holiday had arrived.

Hetty and her friends were invited to a Christmas party at the old wooden hut where she enjoyed her dancing class. Everyone had the most wonderful time. Mrs Evans was sporting a very smart, newly knitted red hat trimmed with tinsel while she played the piano. Afterwards, she handed all the children a little gift bags of sweets from her huge tapestry bag. She really was a very kind lady.

The children had saved some of their pocket money, so they could give her a Christmas present. They gave her a bright new knitting pattern so she could make herself a colourful cardigan, ready for the spring. The children's gift for their dancing teacher was a pink felt case for her glasses — when she eventually took them off from the end of her nose! They were both very happy with their gifts and thanked the children for being so thoughtful.

The party ended with everyone singing…

> We wish you a merry Christmas
> And a happy new year!

Leaving the party, Hetty hugged her friends and they all wished each other a merry Christmas.

"See you all again after the holidays! Have a lovely time!"

Just then, a train went rumbling out of the station. It had a Christmas tree tied to the front of the engine. The engine driver waved to the children and blew the whistle.

"Happy Christmas!" He called out.

The children waved back at him.

Hetty smiled to herself for a moment, remembering her wonderful summer holiday meeting her very own Mr Christmas.

The next day, Hetty helped Mummy decorate the Christmas cake. It looked just perfect, complete with a snowman, sprigs of holly, lots of little silver balls. Finally, they finished it off with a red and gold Christmas band.

Daddy made sure plenty of logs were brought in for the fire. He stacked them high in the basket next to the fireplace.

Everything was now in place, for today was Christmas Eve.

Granny soon arrived to spend Christmas time together. The evening was spent talking about old times, chatting and laughing. Mummy prepared a lovely supper. Then everyone enjoyed a game of Snakes and Ladders while they roasted chestnuts by the fire.

"It is getting very late." Daddy said, thinking it was time for Hetty to get ready for bed.

She did feel quite tired, but also very excited. First, she had to hang up her stocking by the fireplace. Then she left out a freshly baked mince pie for Father Christmas, and a carrot for Rudolf.

"Goodnight Mummy and Daddy," Hetty said on her way up the stairs.

"Sweet dreams," said Granny.

"I wonder if Father Christmas will come down the chimney tonight." Hetty said.

"Well Hetty, you know he only comes when we are all fast asleep," said Mummy, "now off to bed with you…"

The next morning, Hetty gave a big stretch and slowly opened her eyes. It was very, very early. But you are allowed to wake up early on Christmas morning, don't you think? Leaping from her bed, she ran over to her bedroom window.

Sure enough, a light layer of snow had covered the garden. It was as if everything had been dusted in icing sugar. Hetty also noticed there were a new set of footprints that had been left by someone?

I wonder, she smiled.

Creeping quietly from her bedroom, then tip-toeing as quickly as she could down the stairs, Hetty slowly opened the sitting room door.

Under the Christmas tree there were gifts for everyone, also an empty plate where Hetty had left the mince pie and carrot.

She went to look very carefully at the fireplace. She felt quite sure she could see a little sprinkling of…. Yes! Fairy dust.

"Good morning, little one. You are up early," said Granny.

"Oh yes," said Hetty. "Look Granny, Father Christmas has left all these lovely presents under the tree. Do you think it is too early to wake up Mummy and Daddy?"

"It is Christmas morning, everyone loves Christmas morning. Go on Hetty, quickly, what are you waiting for?"

"I do love you Granny, you are the best Grandma in the whole world."

"Good morning," said Daddy. "Happy Christmas, everyone. Mummy is making us all some hot chocolate."

"That sounds lovely," said Hetty.

Everyone gathered happily around the Christmas tree, wrapped up in their cosy dressing gowns with large mugs of hot chocolate.

"Father Christmas has been very busy," said Daddy, "just look at all these gifts!"

"Please can we open some?" Hetty asked.

"Yes, of course you can."

"But just wait a moment," said Granny. "Hetty, don't you think you might have forgotten something very important?"

"Goodness, my pink ribbon! Fairy Fern said I must wear it just for today."

She dashed from the sitting room and up the stairs as fast as she could, leaving Mummy and Daddy mystified as to what was going on.

"This is a very special day for Hetty," said Granny, "and that is all I am going to say."

As soon as Hetty returned, wearing her pink ribbon, the room was suddenly magically bathed in bright light glowing with all the colours of the rainbow.

"This is crazy," said Mummy, "what ever is going on? Oh my goodness, Hetty, just look at your old teddy Bear."

Teddy had suddenly appeared under the Christmas tree. He was dressed in a brand new set of clothes consisting of a very smart bright scarlet red jacket, and trousers made from softest green velvet.

"Granny, don't you think he looks just like a little Pixie?"

Hetty and Granny both started to giggle.

"This is all very strange," said Daddy. "You see, there is a little Robin tapping at the window. How very odd."

Suddenly in a flash of light, a large gift box materialised right before their eyes. It was tied up with the most beautiful scarlet red ribbons.

Granny handed it to Hetty.

"I think this must be a gift for you, my dear."

Before Hetty had chance to open it, the scarlet ribbons magically untied themselves and the box flew open.

"Goodness," gasped Mummy, "what ever will happen next?"

"It is just Christmas magic, that's all." Said Granny.

Hetty peered into the box. She could not believe her eyes, as one by one she gently lifted out seven beautiful tiny little fairy dolls. Each one was dressed in a different colour of the rainbow. And there was something else. A little note inside the box read…

To Our Dearest Hetty,

For you to treasure, seven little fairy dolls
One for each colour of the rainbow
With our love to you always.

From,

All the pixies, fairies, King Frog,
And your very own Mr Christmas.

Maybe someday we might all meet again.
I do hope so, until then please give our love
To your Grandma and dear Uncle Jim.
Always take care of your pink ribbon.
Now your wishes have come true.

Have a very Merry Christmas, Hetty
As without your help, it would never would
have happened.
From,
Your little friend forever
Fern xxx

"Well Mummy and Daddy, I just knew one day I would meet the Fairies. You see, Granny said if I kept wishing and wishing long enough, my wishes might just come true. Now they have, don't you think it is just truly wonderful?"

"Oh yes, Hetty," said Mummy. "Goodness me, you were right all along!"

"Listen," said Daddy, "I am sure I just heard the little fairy on the top of the Christmas tree giggle!"

"Now that is real magic, don't you think?" Hetty smiled.

MERRY CHRISTMAS, EVERYONE

I do hope you've enjoyed
Hetty's magical story...
(who knows, perhaps wishes
really do come true)

Hetty's Dunster

Many years have passed for now Hetty is a Grandma.

But she often returns to visit the lovely village where she spent so many happy holidays as a child.

Not much has changed, sadly Uncle Jims garage behind the Church has been replaced with new houses.

Dunster Castle will always be standing proudly on top of the hill.

The old watermill can still be found at the end of the lane.

Also the bridge over the stream with its little stone seat.

Visit the beautiful Dunster Church, Yarn Market, Dovecote, Secret Garden and Wishing Well... perhaps wishes really come true?

Nothing has changed for hundred of years.

You can still hear the Rooks calling from high up in Conygar
Tower.

With their black feathers black as the darkest night…..

The wonderful old steam train is still taking children on holiday
just like it always has…..

One question you might want to ask…

Did Hetty really meet the Fairies in the Castle Woods?

Who knows!

Or perhaps it was just…

A Village Fairy Tale…

About the Author

I grew up in Taunton, an only child born in 1945 to my loving parents May and Stephen Humphries.

'Toots' was a nickname given to me by my Father. I have always used it as my business name over the years.

Just like Hetty in my story, I would spend many happy summer holidays in magical Dunster staying with my Aunty Lily and Uncle Jim.

Now I must thank my wonderful family and friends who have encouraged me to finally put pen to paper.

I have enjoyed such a busy time bringing up my two daughters and son, who over the years have made me a very proud Grandma to Louis, James, Oliver, Josh, Isabelle, Darcy and little Alexander.

They are the reason I wanted to write Granny's fairy story but I hope you will enjoy it too.

Hullo Creative have been amazing in making it all really happen. Also my dear friend Deenagh Miller, who has made it so magical with her beautiful illustrations. A huge big thank you to you all.

Toots and her Daddy with Dunster Castle in the distance

Toots (far right) with family and friends at Dunster Beach

Ingram Content Group UK Ltd.
Milton Keynes UK
UKHW020658290323
419305UK00002B/33